Una Woods was brought up in
Queen's University in the late 19
became closely involved in the fo
traditional songs. She lived for son
London, where she married, and then returned to Belfast. She has been writing short stories for several years, but *The Dark Hole Days* is her first book. She has two children.

To my Mother
Nancy
She took her dreams quietly . . .

The Dark Hole Days

Una Woods

THE
BLACKSTAFF
PRESS

First published in 1984
by The Blackstaff Press
3 Galway Park, Dundonald, Belfast BT16 0AN
with the assistance of
the Arts Council of Northern Ireland

'X-Days' first appeared in the Irish Press, and
'Cora's Plight' in Northern Life

Printed in Northern Ireland
by The Universities Press Limited

British Library Cataloguing in Publication Data
Woods, Una
The dark hole days
I. Title
823,.[F] PR6073.063/
ISBN 0 85640 316 4

The Dark Hole Days

Wednesday night or Thursday morning 12.15

Madge heard them saying in the taxi going down the road, that it's all about to blow up again. She's not the only one either. People are fed up with initiatives. They don't know what they are. I heard a woman saying why don't they do something real. Most people don't know what.

Went out with Matt tonight. To the pictures. It wasn't much good. I can't even remember the name. I'd rather be somewhere having a chat, but where is there? We walked home and that was good though we were a bit nervous. Mam says when they were going out they used to walk across to the east. It's a bad time. We might move, Dad says, but where would you go?

Brought Matt in but it was mad, with the eight of our ones milling around. You can't get those kids to bed. They want to see everything. Dad was out but came home early. Mam says she doesn't rest till the door's closed and we're all safe.

Our kids have rings round their eyes.

Chuck was in with Dad tonight. He's got all the solutions. He says take the politicians away and let the people get on with sorting it out. Our Pete said sure the people don't agree but Chuck said that's the thing. They only think they don't agree because they listen to the politicians on television telling them they don't agree. Television should be done away with, Chuck says. Television and politicians.

1.00 in the morning

They're still down there. Our kids have finally fallen asleep, and I can hear them talking although Dad doesn't say much. He told me the other day there's too much talking, there are hardly any quiet people around these days. Where's the dignity of the past, he asked me. I couldn't tell him. The only person he really likes listening to is Mam. You wouldn't think she was from Belfast at all, Aunt Sadie used to say. Aunt Sadie's dead.

Thursday 0130 hours

Out with Gerry and Sam getting some information for protection purposes. Learning how not to be selfish. Have learned a lot since I met Gerry and Sam in the dole. There aren't enough people who care, Sam said. I was one. I was just messing around, playing billiards. I let others get on with it. Like politicians. Can politicians protect us, Sam asked me. I said no. We have to protect ourselves, Gerry said. Even the security forces can't. They're not inside. But we are.

Was at a meeting earlier. Can't say much about it. Even to myself. But I'm a part of something now. I have friends and important thoughts about history and the country. I hated history at school. Now I'm in it.

Sam said we might be in action soon. For our protection. He and Gerry and a few others are getting us ready.

I can't say anything about it.

Thursday morning 10.30

Our four away to school. Pete still in bed, Denny at work, Sadie teaching in the nursery school, Madge down in the cafe. Dad gone for the paper and a pint after. I did the usual, helping to get the wee ones out and then a bit of tidying up. Dad was paid off last year, before I kept a diary. I thought of it to fill in time till I get a job. Dad says with six O-levels and two As it's only a matter of time. I'm young. He's not the same since. He liked work, though I'd get bored in a factory. He said it was worth it for the weekends. Now it's all the same, each day, nothing to look forward to. But he doesn't complain much. He likes a visit to the pub in the morning. He has some good friends.

I think of other places. I could go to England. Why would young people stay here? It's dead. It's only for people who can't get out. Yet some come back. They can't stand to be away. Like the Munroes round the corner. Imagine coming back from Australia to that. It's hard to understand it. Matt and me talked about going to America when (if) we get married but there's the possibility that I would wither away amongst strangers. So that's my question answered – why people come back.

I'm looking down on the estate now. It's a weird sort of wilderness, yet in every house there's a story. I think about the stories. Sometimes they are sad and then there's a white flash. It might be a wedding or a christening and white laughing teeth. I think of blacks and whites. If I wrote stories, some would be black and some white.

Thursday 1300 hours

Just had breakfast. Ma said Gerry left word to meet him at Coal bunker. That's code. Ma doesn't like it. She says I've no sense, that God knows who I'll get mixed up with. But she doesn't know anything really. She thinks it's just a game, like gangs when you're a kid. And she likes Sam. He always treats her well. One day he gave her a box of chocolates. It's the first time I saw her blushing. It's the others she doesn't know that she's worried about. I tell her I'm playing billiards most of the time. She's turned against billiards. I said at least I don't drink or take drugs. I don't even smoke. She said that was true.

It doesn't seem so bad not having a job now. I used to lie in bed most of the day.

Off to meet Gerry.

Thursday evening 7.15

Paul broke off with our Madge. Madge ate no tea. She'll be

hanging around all night with a face like the longest day. She's only known him three weeks, but that's our Madge. I might try to get her interested in a game of draughts. On the other hand she may call for Laura Munroe. Laura who talks with an Australian accent even though she was only there for two years. She has a guy there, she says, who's waiting to marry her. I asked her why she didn't stay and she said her mum said good people are needed here, it wouldn't be right to desert it. I asked her what she was doing except working in the cafe with Madge, and she turned up her nose and said spreading sanity around. I hope she's right. Dad laughed when I imitated her to him but he said, Oh they're alright, the Munroes. Harmless people. Maybe that's all we need.

I've tried on three jumpers and I don't know what to wear with these green trousers. Not that it matters. Me and Matt'll probably just have a wee walk up the road.

Thursday 2005 hours

Down by the embankment. Autumn colours made me think of Da's funeral. It was blowing hard and leaves were swirling in our faces. I remember Uncle George's big heavy coat. It was the fashion then with a thick belt and big lapels. He asked me to come under it, for my face was blue. I refused. Ma had on a black coat she borrowed from Mimi Roberts. It was too long. Why didn't she wear her own? Dark blue would have been alright. You can't talk to Ma.

Friday 0100 hours

God you want to have seen them all tonight. I can't believe it's real. I think I'm dreaming or maybe watching a film, but then I realise it's me there with all the lads. Got a glimpse of the boss but he had a mask. Sam said he can't afford to take chances, even in front of us. There's always traitors and it might be who you least expect. It could even be you, he said to me. It gave me an eerie feeling but then he burst out laughing and I laughed too. We're all together.

Friday 2.35 in the morning

Beat our Madge at draughts, two to one, but then our Sadie beat me two to nil. So what does that prove? I'm better than Madge but Sadie's better than me. I strolled up the road a bit with Matt. He seems depressed, what with no work, and this place. He might go to England to his brother. He's a carpenter. Matt could work for him. He says what's keeping me here, but I don't know. I'd have to think about it. Sometimes I think even though I love Matt, I should take some time to myself. If I went with him now I'd be giving myself over, wouldn't I? But then what do I want to do? I wouldn't mind writing some of these stories I think about. Achieve something on my own. Maybe even earn some decent money. Now that wouldn't be bad. I was looking at a suit the other day. It was made up of lovely autumny shades. I could see me strolling in the country in that suit. I showed it to Teresa but she apparently found it amusing. Who do you think you are, she said. It's not exactly the moon I'm asking for but surely all my dreams don't end here: me in a duffle coat signing on the dole and walking in the debris of Belfast. Then again I look at Mam, so at home with herself, and I think, why should I want more. Or different. She impresses me. She's part of ongoing life, or something like that.

It's a predicament.

Saturday 1900 hours

In town all afternoon. So much going on you wouldn't believe it. I'm sure it's like every other city. Except me and Gerry and Sam walking through Smithfield knew we had a secret. Gerry bought tapes, the Police and others. Says he might have a party and would I like to come. Would I not! Sam disappeared for half an hour. Me and Gerry dandered round. I looked at some fishing tackle. Might take it up with Uncle George. But not now. Later, when there's time. When it's all over. It will be all over, Sam and Gerry say. They know things that I don't know – yet. But once you're in, Sam says. I looked at myself in a shop window and liked a new kind of serious look in my eyes. I always thought I would be something. Maybe an actor. Sometimes it feels like that. Sam brought back fish and chips. We ate them beside Kavanagh's. There was too much vinegar. Still it was good. You know that wintery feeling. Gerry saw a girl he fancies but Sam said there'll be plenty of time for all that. Anyway Gerry said he wouldn't go after her with the smell of fish and chips.

The shops were lighting up when we walked home.

Saturday evening 8.30

Missed last night but not much happened. Mam and Dad went to the club together. We persuaded them because they don't go out together enough. Eddie Stewart left them home and Chuck called in to hear the gossip. We managed to get all the wee ones into bed to give them peace. Mam likes the men around – but don't take that up the wrong way. Pete came home about twelve. Dad's worried about his drinking. Madge and Laura spent the night looking through catalogues. The things they're sending away for! You'd look daft in them around these parts. Laura says they're for wearing back to the outback and Madge is talking about going with her. Our Sadie was out with John. When she came in she made us all tea. Then she sat and read. Sadie's the quiet one, the discreet one. Dad calls her the thinker. What's our Sadie thinking about us now, he says. She smiles like a lady. Our Madge is jealous.

Went down the town this afternoon. I like Saturdays in the town. I went an hour before I was to meet Matt so as to walk about a bit myself. The suit was gone but maybe there are more inside. Walked around by North Street and through Smithfield. The music coming from the record shops somehow gave me a feeling of freedom and made me imagine I was going to do things – interesting and adventurous. I think really I must leave Belfast at some stage. The more I think of it the more it seems I could not justify spending my life in this corner. But it's all very vague. Like trying to make a decision when the alternatives aren't yours to begin with. Are there possibilities? When I look back I'll say, at nineteen you must have had possibilities. From here they're in a mist. Trying to find your way in a fog. When the fog lifts it was all so clear after all.

The other evening Denny had a ladybird on his arm. One of the kids went to swat it but Denny said, Hey you, that ladybird's life is as important as yours. He went to put it outside but he dropped it. Ah, it's gone, he said, groping round the floor. Oh well, he said, and sat down again. Our kids all roared laughing. I mentioned that because it struck me, although I'm not sure why. I'll read it later and maybe something will click.

Met Matt in White's cafe. Had a cup of tea and a doughnut, and Matt had coffee. He looked well. Nicely dressed and in good form. His brother says Birmingham's great. You can do what you want in your own flat and at night you don't have to worry about anything. How would you like a weekend in Birmingham, Matt asked me. I might, I said.

And I might.

Sunday 0200 hours if the clock's right

Shattered, but in a satisfied way. Sam's very happy with my progress. You're doing well kid, he said to me. After practice I was in the flat of a friend of his. Vera. Something going on there, though she looks no chicken to me. Still, not bad in the figure. I'd say Sam would have no problem there. She made us coffee. I felt a bit out of it when they left me with a pile of Jim Reeves LPs. I'd never heard of the guy and have no wish to again. Heard noises from the other room which made me wish I had a girl beside me there on the couch. Never really had a girl, well, not serious. At that point I wouldn't have said no to Vera and her Jim Reeves LPs.

Sam cheered me up when we were walking home. What I like about you kid, he said, is that you're the dedicated sort. It's true. I always was.

Sunday afternoon 5.20

Sunday dreary Sunday. When, if, I get some control the first thing I'll do is change Sunday. It deserves a good shaking at the least. Is it different in other places or do people everywhere sit around in their good clothes waiting for nothing to happen? Some thoughts. Are we dressed up for God's entertainment or are we clinging to tradition? Do we need to be freed from it all or should we find an alternative first? Was any of it ever good or did it only distract us?

After dinner, which takes up most of the day anyhow, we spend the rest of the time bumping into each other. Madge and Sadie have resorted to the draughts, but only in a half-interested way. I'm glad to sneak away to this. Roll on Monday.

Sunday 1900 hours

Sam and Gerry not available on Sundays. That's a rule. I usually sleep late. Ma gets the dinner which we eat silently or Ma might say, Now just content yourself around the house for today. Sometimes I walk through the park and meet up with some of the old mates although I haven't much time for idle chat these days. There's no meaning. Today I went out alone. I had a sense of power and even superiority. Ma tried to talk to me at tea. Things about Mimi Roberts' husband and holidays and Mimi's bad leg that she has to lift onto the bus. I said, Aye it's terrible right enough. I suppose she used to tell Da. Then she asked me did I not notice the new heels on my brown boots. I lied that I did. What do you want for your birthday next week, she said. I've just thought of a shirt. I'll go down and tell her a blue shirt, or she might end up getting me another white one.

Monday evening 6.30

We've been very worried about wee Dan. He hasn't been himself and the doctor's sending him to the hospital for tests. I can hardly look at him for fear it's something serious. I feel it's a threat and everything could change for us overnight. Maybe I'm just a pessimist. Mam and Sadie are sensibly controlling their feelings. I'm thinking to myself, life will be difficult if I fall apart so readily. After all he's only going for tests, I'd better catch myself on.

Still I'm looking forward to seeing Matt tonight. The people closest to you are the ones who matter. It's a question of developing, keeping those relationships. Why look beyond that? Or is that selfish or narrow? I don't know.

I can hear Sadie singing to Dan. Why is she singing to Dan? She's singing to Dan because she knows he likes it. She's not wrapping herself up in her own anxiety. I'm going to try.

Monday 1915 hours

Gerry seemed concerned, as if he was miles away. And he asked me a strange thing. What do you think you'd have done if you'd lived in a different time? I said how do I know and anyway I like it now. Then he said, or if you'd been rich, up the Malone Road, or something? Did you ever think of that, he said. I said no, can't say I ever did. I do, he said. I don't believe him. Gerry's not the sort to think. You know what we'll end up doing, Gerry, I told him. Protecting the people up the Malone Road. That's what I told him. Will we, he asked me. He looked at me, sensing the importance of my words. We will, I said and he shook his head. He was amazed. Sometimes I can't believe the things I come out with these days. I've got a future.

Tuesday 12.50 in the morning

Had a close night with Matt. We went up the road for a walk and called in for one drink. You wouldn't believe the drinking that goes on. Tables and glasses and waiters falling over themselves and the sad ones at the bar. I wonder who's at home waiting for them night after night. When I was a child I used to walk in the middle of the road passing a pub. One day in Royal Avenue I heard the awful thud of a drunk man's head on the pavement. People around said the drink'll save him. He won't feel it the same as if he was sober.

I was relieved when we came into the air and when we were walking down I had this feeling again, that what I have is as good as anybody could hope for. But I'm guilty and embarrassed about that feeling. As if that's a thought for old age. Not now. I haven't earned it.

Madge is complaining about the light. She's raging because she hasn't been able to sneak a look at this. I told her it's only a diary and she said, I hope there's nothing about me in there. I said don't be daft, I only write about important things – which she did not appreciate. Our Sadie is sleeping. Goodnight Madge. Madge is a bit of a problem. But then, what does she think of me? What does anyone think of me?

Tuesday 0120 hours

Can't say anything about tonight. The lads, you know. But it's under control. Ma waited up. Says I'm prowling about like a foreigner and to take that look off my face. The radio was on when I came in. Old dance music and she was dressed up, that blue dress she used to wear when she and Da went dancing. Now what's she up to? I've been dancing, son, she said with a peculiar smile and she tried to twirl me in the kitchen. Give us a break, I said and came up the stairs. It's not long since you used to have a wee dance with me, she shouted up from the bottom of the stairs. It seems a long time to me. And you used to shine your Daddy's black shoes, do you remember that? Aye, I said, but I don't think she heard me. I might have a word with Mimi Roberts about her tomorrow if I've time. Right enough she's always polishing at them few cups my Da and her won. Hope she's alright but I can't let it get in the way of the bigger good. As Sam says, we're only insects but some are more important insects than others.

Wednesday afternoon 4.15

Watching the evening light, the sunset, from my window. I used to wish I was from the country. I couldn't get over the stillness across the fields and the slow talk of country people. I thought my appreciation could make it mine. I sat on a bridge one day and thought, this is part of me. But you can't start from what you're not. I'm a city person. A suburban girl. That's what I am.

Great news about Dan. The specialist found nothing and he's picked up already. A big weight is lifted off us. Dad has him down in the park. He was bouncing up and down on Dad's shoulders delighted with the fuss that's being made of him.

I have just finished a very good book. It made me think there's a fair chance I'll settle to write sometime. I'd like to capture a quality of ordinary life or something. That book did it.

Mam took a turn down the town on her own. She used to go with Aunt Sadie. Aunt Sadie made a big issue of it, with her fur coat and brown felt hat with a feather on it. Mam used to say somehow she was out of place on the bus, kicking away the rubbish under her seat and poking in her purse for the fare. Soon after the start of the troubles they stopped the routine. Aunt Sadie said things will never be the same again. Dad used to call her a wee china doll. So straight and uppity without anything to be uppity about, and her little bulgy cheeks all powdered and rouged and her poppy eyes. But, as Chuck says, it's the outlook that counts. It was a shock when she died upright in her floral-covered chair. She had the *Irish Times* on her knee. It just shows you, Chuck said. You never know what secrets people have. Chuck took it badly. It was rumoured that he'd been saving for years to ask her to marry him. She would never have married Chuck. Not when he wears dungarees and drinks out of a black mug.

There's our Sadie calling me for tea and the sun's gone down.

Wednesday 2348 hours

Rock on, what's the latest. I can't tell me. Sam and Gerry had other business. Suggested I stay in house till I got word to come. Ma got the wrong impression and got the Ludo out at which point I reminded her I'm not a child any more. That hurt her. You know Ludo's not like Snakes and Ladders, she said. I played one game to please her. She kept getting sixes and fives and I got ones and twos. I didn't even get my last man out. She laughed and said, you remember I used to give you chances when you were young? You're too old for chances now. If Sam and Gerry saw me they'd die.

Sam sent his kid brother at ten. Ma said she was just making me chips and a tin of red salmon, a big tin. Bring all your friends round, we'll have a bit of a night, she said. I told her, It's a man's world, Ma. To please her I said maybe we'll go to Butlin's next year and asked her to brush the back of my jacket.

Sam's kid tried to get some info from me but I had no trouble dealing with that. Lay off kid, I said. Me and Sam's got business to attend to. That's what I said. Lay off kid.

Met Sam in Hanky-Panky Alley (code). Sam was walking up and down. He put his arm round my shoulder. Talked. That's all I'm prepared to say. Gerry arrived. Gerry's got a worried look. Maybe Gerry's not up to it. But, as Sam says, once you're in. When we parted, as Gerry and Sam were walking up the other way, I watched after them. Sam was talking into Gerry's face and I heard Gerry saying, Okay, I've got it. Got it. Sam's a born leader. He could talk you into anything.

The salmon was okay but the chips were cold and Ma was asleep in the chair.

Wednesday night or Thursday morning 12.50

Matt's serious. About us going to Birmingham for the weekend. We'd get the ferry and train. Pool our doles. What would Mam and Dad think about that? I will have to put it to them tomorrow. Matt wants to do it soon. Can't deny I'm getting excited in more ways than one. The thought of branching out, just lifting up, almost like flying, even for a couple of days. But then, how can you be free within those limits? If you know you're coming back. Will the coming back ruin it from the start? Chuck says freedom does not exist or it does. If it does you could be in prison and it will still be yours. If it doesn't you could be sailing round the world and be a prisoner. Chuck sets us thinking. He should have been something. He gets the odd job polishing for people but, as he says, it's more fashionable now not to have your wood polished. Nobody's interested in specialists these days. It's a ram-stam world. That's another of Chuck's opinions. Dad says he should have a book published – 'Chuck's Views in Alphabetical Order'. It would be a best-seller, he says. Dad's the opposite. He keeps it all to himself.

Sadie and Mam are talking downstairs. I've a feeling Sadie will marry John next year after he finishes university. Everything will be proper and smooth. Sadie has already thought of the answer before you ask her a question. She looks in as though from a height. She'll leave Belfast with John or they will live around the university and shop in Botanic Avenue. Sadie will dress well and everyone who knows her will taste the better side of life.

Now our Madge. I can hear her banging things away in the kitchen. Looking for notice. Maybe she'll pull out of it. She's a year younger than me. Sadie is two years older. Madge does weird things like wearing big woollen socks with a long skirt. She says she's different, and she's always listening to the radio and humming to herself. She criticises Mam and Dad and says there's no fire in them. I don't know what she expects after nine children. She sits on the kitchen table swinging her legs and eating jam doughnuts which she sends the young ones for. She's plump and no wonder. It doesn't help matters. She started doing exercises but she said they made her hungry and it was necessary to send for more jam doughnuts. She's not the most refined of people. Our Pete says he'd prefer to be served in a cafe by the Incredible Hulk any day.

Eddie Stewart called with the news that our Barney's been mitching school. It's not easy for a fourteen-year-old lad. The teachers don't understand. They just see you as a pupil, not a person who has another life behind. Sometimes they clash, especially today. Barney says he can't concentrate and he's punished for not doing his homework. But I saw him trying. It's not easy with so many in the house. Our Barney is a nice kid but he's getting moody. Here's Madge. I'd better hide this.

Friday 1350 hours

Signed on. The faces in that dole queue. You'd think they were lining up for the last judgement and not too sure about where they'd be put. Some people have nothing to look forward to. Their eyes show it, just staring at the next man's back and not even seeing it. It used to get me down when I was one of them. And then the odd Cheerful Charlie who tries to liven them up. But it's all out of place – like shouting in the church. And there's me and Sam and Gerry who have something to do. Even the girl behind the desk knows I'm not just like the man in front. She respects me. One day she almost said something to me, the way she opened her mouth. But she couldn't, with the queue and everything, and then she wouldn't be sure if I would have time. Isn't it funny how the way you feel changes the way you look. She can see my dignity. I might pass her a note some time telling her I'll take her out. I like that spotted blouse, the tight one, and the way her hair just touches her breast. She's not like some of the others who treat the men like dirt. She's nice. I could see us down at the embankment or even on Vera's couch. I would tell Sam she's okay.

She's okay but if she was my girl I'd get her out of that place. I'd show her there's more to life than lines of men in donkey jackets queueing to write their names.

Met Sam. Only a word. Not good to be seen too much together during the day, Sam said. Will call me later. Had a chat with Gerry in the street. Did you hear the latest, Gerry asked me. What latest, I said. On the political side, he said. No, I said, never listen to those guys these days. Some joke, Gerry said and went on. I came in and asked Ma. She likes the news. Och, she said, another one of them what-do-you-call-thems. What, I said. Och you know, she said, it begins with 'in'. After a while I guessed – initiatives. Aye, them things, Ma said and went on cleaning the cups. Is that all, I said, and came up here. As Sam says, they haven't a clue.

There's a cold wind. Hope the stars are out tonight. We'll be on the hill looking down on the lights of the city. There it is, the boss said, that's what we're defending. Ma will be sitting up at the fire, which reminds me I must fill the coal bucket. Don't forget the hero's always good to women, so long as they don't get in the way of his work.

Friday afternoon 2.45 or thereabouts

Laura Munroe's mother bought thirty tins of baked beans this morning. They're for the siege, she said. She was fuming when somebody accused her of buying up everything and leaving nothing for others. How dare you, she said. My house will be an open door when the time comes. Maggie Denver thought it was a great joke. We'll be alright now, she shrieked, as long as there's beans at Munroe's. But what I want to know, she added, is who's going to provide the toast?

Chuck and Dad came in together. Chuck issued immediate advice that we were not to listen to the gossip-mongers. The gossip-mongers and the press are panickers, he said. If we listened to all they had to say, we might as well not get out of our beds in the morning. Dad and he and Mam set about discussing it. How they create a dangerous climate and make life more difficult for the rest of us. Mam said, Well let us deal in fact, which is hard enough to take, God knows, and leave fiction for those who need it. Madge left the kitchen at this point, saying was it any use her having the Archers on if she couldn't hear a damned word they were saying. Dad got up to go after her for her lack of manners but Chuck said who could blame the child for trying to escape into a world of petty happenings. She still has dreams, he said. Sometimes this house is nuts. The next thing they were all singing 'Beautiful Dreamer'. When they had finished I thought it might be the moment to discuss my dreams of a weekend in Birmingham. I purposely raised it in front of Chuck, hoping for his support. But Chuck can be unpredictable. Birmingham's a dump, he said. He then launched an attack on anyone who hadn't appreciated the fact that he'd worked his guts out in the slums of Birmingham and other such places for the British economy. What thanks did he get, he asked us. None, I said, knowing by his tone that this was the case. I worked my way up to the scrap heap, he said, and his head sank on his chest at a melancholy angle. I left the room, as this was not the reaction I had hoped for.

Nothing will stop me going to Birmingham. Too many people are living with regrets. The best course you can take, I've decided, is to do what you think you should do when you think you should do it. Then at least, whatever happens, you'll have the satisfaction of knowing you did it.

Keeping a diary is good. I can react to my own thoughts.

Saturday 0330 hours

A bit muddled. Try a drink, Sam said, but I didn't really get through it. Maybe not, Sam said, on second thoughts. It was in Vera's. Remember Vera is a friend, Sam said. If you're ever in trouble, come here. Vera was standing in her dressing gown when I arrived. It was slung round and tied. Royal blue. I'd nipped home to tell Ma not to worry, I was back. Sam said nip round to Vera's after if you like. Ma wanted to know how come I'm away again if I'm back. I'm just finishing off a game, you go on to bed, I told her. When I was going down the hall she said, son, you're all I've got. I'll definitely have to see Mimi Roberts about her.

Vera thought I'd need a coffee so Sam left on an errand. Does Gerry ever come here, I asked Vera. Son, they all come here, she said, even you. She started sort of rolling over to me on the couch. I told her I liked her dressing gown. I was nervous the way she was doing it and all. She's a grown woman. I moved away. Sam should be back any minute, I said and stood up. But she was up like a shot and not allowing me an inch against the wall. I look after Sam, don't worry, she sort of murmured. It's funny, I said, Sam strikes me as the sort who can look after himself. You know what I mean, cheeky, she said. She pulled my ears and I had no choice but to get back on the couch. I was terrified out of my mind when she flapped open the dressing gown. I'm waiting for the girl from the dole, I shouted. This got to her because she pulled herself together. Finish your coffee, she said. She put on a Jim Reeves LP and was singing away in the kitchen when Sam came back. Sam looked at me. I was glad I hadn't stolen his woman. Vera came out and leant against the kitchen door. She winked at Sam. Sam laughed. I laughed.

But I'm not sure about it all. I think it was a test and I don't know if I passed or failed. Maybe they're too smart for me. But then why would they waste their time on me?

By the way, my birthday.

Saturday afternoon 1.15

It's decided. Next weekend. Dad was doubtful but was persuaded a weekend out of this place could only be good. Sadie said I could borrow some of her clothes and Madge said I'll have a rotten time. Pete told me to look out for a job for him. I'll do anything, he said. Tell them that.

Barney was sent home for fighting yesterday. Dad says it's hopeless. He's quite depressed about it. How can you correct somebody without offering them hope? What can he tell our Barney? He's going up to see the Principal anyway, to talk. Barney's out hanging about somewhere.

Chuck says somebody has to do something. When Pete sighed and said, We've heard that before, Chuck was on his feet. No, he said, I mean really. Really, something completely new. When are they going to realise there's no hope in any of this? What do you suggest, Dad asked him. At this point everyone was looking as though nothing had any point to it. Everyone except Chuck, that is. Do you know what I've been thinking, he said. Divide the people. A new partition, but not of places, of people. Because, the way I see it, until everybody realises you can't change people's minds we'll get nowhere. Pete went to interrupt but Chuck was in one of his excitements. Nowhere, he repeated. So here's what we do. We let those who want to belong to Britain be ruled by the British government, and those who choose to be ruled by the Republic of Ireland be governed by the Southern government. Pete said that's rubbish, and I asked how it could be worked. How do you expect me to know, Chuck said. It's not up to me to work out the details. Dad said anything new is worth a try at this stage, but there are those who will accept nothing. And yet, Mam said, if they had a decent job there's many who'd leave it at that.

All the people's thoughts. Ideas floating and clashing and breaking and falling and out of the dust another spark, another thought.

Another man was shot today.

Saturday 1829 hours

My birthday. Got the shirt. Blue with white stripes and a card from Ma to her loving son. Mimi Roberts got me a tie to match. I'll wear them tomorrow, I promised Ma, and we'll visit Uncle George and Aunt Jo-Jo. Ma's fussing around flapping her wings like a big hen. Makes me feel I've just hatched out of an egg. I'm the ugly duckling, all awkward and out of place, only Ma doesn't notice. She baked me a cake and put candles on it and her and Mimi sang Happy Birthday. Ma cried and said not to mind her, she'd cried every year since I was born. Then she twiddled the radio knobs until she found dance music and her and Mimi waltzed. They tried to get me up but I said I'd probably end up walking on Mimi's bad leg or something. Don't worry, Ma laughed, we'll have the great nights when he brings a nice wee girl home. I'd love to see their faces if I strolled in with Vera. What a laugh. They're prancing about down there still. Some pair.

Never mentioned it to Sam and Gerry. What's a birthday?

They didn't show up in town. Must have had important business. Smithfield seemed empty without them but I bought chips and listened to music and thought about the times we're having.

They'll send for me tonight.

2350 hours

Strange. Got a message to go to Starker's Strip (code). When I got there there were a few hanging about, but not Sam. Someone's coming to talk to us, they said. Must be important. A weird feeling. Everybody was afraid to say anything to everybody else, not being sure who we were, in case you said the wrong thing. Nobody arrived to talk to us and about eleven we started to drift out. We're being watched, Gerry said. That's it, another guy agreed. And a bloke said, you see that's the whole point of it.

Haven't seen Sam all day, and tomorrow's Sunday. When I came in early Ma said, I'm glad you made a special effort on your birthday. Wasn't it a great party?

Sure was Ma. A party and a half. Pity Mimi's leg played up, she said after me up the stairs. Pity indeed.

Saturday night or Sunday morning 12.40

Matt and I talked about our plans. He got the tickets today.

We'll go on the ferry on Friday night to Heysham. It can be a bit rough with drunks and seasickness and that, Matt says, but we'll try to find a wee corner. We walked up the road and talked. Matt's so earnest about everything. We kept each other warm against the night and I had a feeling that together we can reach the centre of something. How can I explain? Well, instead of reaching upwards or outwards, maybe the search should be inwards. I'm not sure, but it's all there already. It's just yourself. The other day I was looking at a simple scene, just the blue sky and white clouds puffing by, and birds drifting easily across. But it gave me a lovely surge of contentment.

Why should I let Matt go? He understands me. Can there be many who understand me? It's just that sometimes in my mind I see myself alone, striding in an unknown place and being in control. Me, of this time. Sitting in a cafe looking out through the window, fashionably dressed but deep. Take note, you people passing by. Remember this moment. Matt wouldn't fit in there. No, he would lessen my presence.

Dad was out for an hour with Chuck and Eddie Stewart. They brought Pete back. Dad was depressed. If you'd seen him up there, Sarah, he said. Sitting at the counter staring at the bottles. You wouldn't have thought there was one belonging to him. God, does that mean our Pete's one of the sad ones?

Chuck said don't worry, we'll nurse him through this bad patch. He's just lost his dignity for a while. Dad's worried in case he did the wrong thing keeping our Pete in at night and that. It was only to keep him out of trouble, he told Chuck. But now he hasn't really any friends. Chuck said, it's only that you've a family of individuals around you. They'll find their way.

Met Teresa in town today. She envies me getting away for the weekend. She says I won't want to come back. People from all over the world live in Birmingham but it's nothing like London. London is the world. Teresa's cousin lives in London. When she comes home on holiday she's always talking about the bloke upstairs and the bloke downstairs. You should see her clothes, Teresa says. She's a secretary. She has to wear something different every day. According to Teresa.

Belfast would fit into a corner of London. Not that it would fit in.

Sunday 1910 hours

When I walked into that there saloon, gee, ya wanna seen them. Afraida turn their heads, their hands ashakin' before ma mighty presence. A slid ma glass down that there counter an' ya never seen anything like the way that there barman jumped. An' when ah left know what ah heard them say? He never even told us his name.

Spent the afternoon in Aunt Jo-Jo's. Me and Uncle George talked a bit about life. Think he feels responsible for me since I've no Da. He said to me, son, you know one day all this will be over and you and I will be left, we hope. I know what my life consists of, but yours, what's yours going to be? I said, What exactly do you mean Uncle George, I'm no different to the fellows anywhere else. Maybe not, son, he said, maybe not. I looked into his face and saw his innocence. And you know, I felt sorry for him. We went for a stroll just as dusk was falling, through the streets and down to the river. We looked into the water and talked about the reflections and he told me my Da and him spent many's the hour racing along the banks and playing cowboys. In our bare feet and braces, son. His face looked old in the grey light and I felt sorry for him again. I wanted to tell him I was working for him but I couldn't. As we walked back I thought it's all the more noble not to boast.

When we got back to the house Ma and Aunt Jo-Jo had the table set. They stood back and Aunt Jo-Jo said how she just could not get over how well I looked. We had our tea and I offered to feed the cat.

Ma and me came home in the bus. Uncle George stood at the stop waving after us. Ma said it was a lovely day. When we got off the bus I raced on down to the house in case there was a message for me. There wasn't.

I didn't expect one on a Sunday.

Sunday evening 7.30

Sunday again. I spent most of this Sunday wondering what next Sunday will be like. Can't imagine it – Sunday out of Belfast. I made lists today of what to take. Eddie Stewart's leaving us to the boat. Our wee ones are asking me to bring them something back. I don't know how I'll manage that, although Dad says he has a few pounds by and he'll give me something. Hope you're not eloping, he said to Matt. Because we want to be there when the day comes. It made me feel a bit uncomfortable. I'm so immersed. I'd like to please them but sometimes it's as though I can't see properly from in here. Maybe next weekend will make things clearer.

Might get my hair cut this week, though not short. What way would you like it, I asked Matt. The way it is, he said. Mam said my fringe would be better shorter. Maybe a bit.

Our Denny finished a chest of drawers today. He's very handy. Always working on something. Pete says, so what, anybody could hammer a few nails into a lump of wood. Denny said that's not the point – anybody didn't do it – I did it.

Pete and Madge are alike. In a way they feel they've nothing to offer. They have just the same as me, the same as Sadie. Only they can't see it. Sadie's always had confidence in herself. And me? I knew there were possibilities. With writing this I feel they may be opening up. And if I never do anything, at least I'll have this. It's an extra me. I've created an extension. Sometimes I think I love it so I can escape into its meaning. But in another way I'm ashamed of it, like I'm ashamed to cry or I'd be humiliated if somebody walked into my room and I had nothing on. How can I describe it? The rawness or something. You know what I mean?

I told Matt we shouldn't see each other on Sundays but I could give him no reason that made sense. He says he needs to see me especially on Sunday, it's such a lonely day. I hear him downstairs. We'll have a wee walk, I suppose, and come back and share some of Sadie's cheese on toast. Or he might want me to go over to his house. Sometimes we get a room to ourselves.

Monday 1815 hours

Gerry called this afternoon. Thought we should go out and have a chat. We went to a club he belongs to. He drank beer. I said a couple of shandies will do me no harm, but I must be sure to keep my wits about me. What do you think of this place, Gerry asked me. It's a fine place, Gerry, I said. A fine place, now what's the problem? No problem, Gerry answered, only, what do you think of Sam? What do I think of Sam, I said. It was a bit of a surprise, him coming out with that. He was taking a chance, I would have thought. But I had no trouble with my answer. I think Sam's a genius, a leader of men, I said. Gerry appeared thoughtful, rubbing his beard and sipping away slowly. I see, he said, a leader of men. Then he turned to me. What about women, he asked me. Out of the blue like that. Women? I said. Yes women, you know, and he made a shape in the air. I know what they are, I said. What about them? He said nothing more but kept staring at me. As far as I know, I continued, Sam is a one-woman man. A one-woman man, he repeated. Are you by any chance referring to Vera? Yes, I said, Vera, that's right, Vera. I was drinking away casually at my shandy, thinking to myself how careless Gerry was, talking like this in a public place, when it came to my notice that his cheeks were bulging and he was trying not to laugh. I stood up at this point, feeling my presence was no longer useful. If it's alright with you, I'll leave now, I said. Sure, Gerry answered, that's alright.

Gerry's a peculiar type, though I wouldn't mention it, not even to Sam.

When I came in Ma met me in the hall. I was just going out to the door to watch for you, she says. Why, I asked her. I walked past and into the kitchen. You know what Mimi Roberts was telling me? she said. Mimi says she wouldn't trust the ones that's playing billiards these days. I was rinsing my hands under the tap. Where's the towel, I asked her. Behind the door where it always is, she says. There's none there, I said. What? She didn't believe me until she looked for herself. My God, she said and scurried off to the hot press. Mimi Roberts doesn't know everything, I shouted after her. Between puffing back down the stairs she said, Nobody knows everything, but some people know a lot, and Mimi Roberts has contacts. Contacts? I took the towel from her. It was nice and warm. Now, she said, all pleased with herself, don't you be so sure of yourself in future. What are you talking about, Ma, I said, but she had her head in the oven getting my dinner out.

When I was eating away at it she stood over me. She nearly always does that, in case I need the salt passed or something. Your oul' Ma hasn't her head in the sand, she said. Just remember that.

There's no good me talking to Mimi Roberts about her if that's the sort of talk Mimi Roberts is coming out with. I'll just carry on regardless. It's my quiet importance they don't understand. My rise from nothing.

Anyway I'd better get ready. I've got somewhere to go.

Monday night 11.52

A word before midnight. Laura Munroe has disappeared. She hasn't been seen since yesterday. The police and everybody are looking for her. They're working on the theory that she has run away. Still, it's dangerous these days. Madge is wandering about as if she's the star of a show or something because she was the last one to see Laura. They went down to Ken's chippy last night. Madge has told the story a hundred times but it's not really much of a clue. She was fed up, Madge says. She told me she was fed up. She misses that guy from Australia. We got a bit of a shock when Mrs Munroe said there is no guy from Australia. It's all in Laura's mind, she said. That's what's wrong with our Laura. She's a dreamer. She imagines things that aren't there at all. Mrs Munroe is in an awful state. We all promised if Laura's found we'll not pretend we know about the guy. But I wouldn't depend on our Madge, she gives the impression she's gloating. There was a photo of Laura in tonight's *Telegraph*. Laura's Dad hired a car and he and Dad drove around most of the day looking for her. Our Madge went with them. it's getting very worrying, going into a second night. Madge says she's going down to the local radio station to make an appeal for her friend to return.

Tuesday morning 11.15

Laura was picked up on the airport road. It was an awful night and she was sitting on a bank along the road, soaked and shivering. She hardly seemed to remember who she was or where she'd been. The man who picked her up said she just kept saying, I've got to get out of here. He took her to the police station. Mrs Munroe was over here a while ago. She says Laura's in bed resting, and at the moment they can't say much about it. The doctor gave her a sedative. Madge is down in the dumps, as if she almost had importance but it faded before she could grasp it. And, after all, it's Laura who's the centre of attention and Madge is away down to Ken's cafe to serve teas as usual.

I can see Laura bogged down. She tasted a bigger possibility and then she was led back here when she was too young to decide. For a while, I suppose, it was a novelty but now what are her options? Something will have to be done for Laura. Something will have to be done for Madge. Something will have to be done for Pete. Something will have to be done for Barney. Barney's the luckiest. For the others it may be too late.

Mam and I are taking a turn in the town when Dad comes in. I'll pick up a few bits and pieces for Birmingham. I can't imagine life now without the prospect of Birmingham. My little bored brain is churning out all sorts of ideas. It will have the responsibility if things go wrong. I'll never forgive it. I'll beat it back to its limits if it takes me beyond the physical possibilities. Does that mean anything? I wonder.

Tuesday 1335 hours

Not long up. Didn't report last night. Well I did, but not to me. Had a game of billiards in the hall. Some of the old mates but, although I'm for them, I'm beyond them in a way. It's difficult. Only my nobility carries me through at such times. It's a question of quality. I mean, it would be easy to be a bully, but this is different. I feel a better person than them but I wouldn't treat them roughly. Some of us are chosen to stand out, and when I watched them last night talking to each other about nothing, I could hardly understand or remember what their lives are about. I nearly despised them but then I recognised my duty to win something back for them.

There's the difference. When I came in, Ma said Sam had called. Did he leave a message? I asked her to which she replied that she wasn't sure he wanted me at all. He accepted a cup of tea and a buttered soda farl, she said, and we had a great chat altogether about the olden times. Sam's not old, I said to her. He may not be, she says, but he has the wit to know what's in a woman's soul. Not like most these days who couldn't string two words together that make sense at all, let alone get to the core of the matter. I asked her again what did he say and finally she admitted – well he did say one thing. What was that, I asked her. She was straightening the covers on the couch and taking her time about answering me. She likes to play it cool sometimes, especially when she thinks she has a secret. Well? I asked her. Oh, yes, she said. Wait till I get it right now, and if she didn't sit down on the couch and stare across at the window as if her memory was floating somewhere there, or on out in the yard. Now what was it? Yes, it was – The waters may separate man from his destiny for a time, but undefeated his spirit will return to raise those who waited in hope. Is Sam going away? I asked her. She shook her head and when she went past me into the kitchen she tapped me on the cheek. In ways you're still a child, she said. She was getting my goat up now. Well, what does it mean then, I said after her, you tell me. Well, she said, it wasn't so much the words. It was the way he said them. In the name of God, Ma, I said, did he tell you to tell me that or what. I was afraid it might be somewhere I was to go. Son, she said, I can't remember that he mentioned your name. Then she went off humming one of those old-time songs.

It's just that you don't understand Sam's cleverness, I said.

And what's more, I know exactly what he meant. I wonder what she thought of that? As for me, there was no need to act on such unreliable information. Sam found I wasn't at home and he decided to humour Ma. Still, I'm sorry I missed him. It mightn't look good. I'll take a walk around later and see if I can run into him. Anyway, I'm thinking of waiting outside for the girl at the dole. I feel I could approach her today.

Tuesday evening 7.40

I liked Mam's plaid coat. We had tea in White's cafe. It's easy to feel she'll always be there. It doesn't change. Not that she should be, but that you know she would. And yet in another way, I wanted to be detached. To have been doing just that, but from a stronger position of my own. Sitting opposite her with my own statement.

The town was normal enough. We peeked into Ken's chippy. Mam said, for God's sake don't let her see us. There she was, hanging over the counter gazing into some bloke's jaw. I'm sure all he wanted was a plate of chips. Madge says you could deep-fry chips of some of the faces you see in there. His did not appear to be one of them. He was good-looking and Madge was making no bones about it. We hurried on.

We had a table near the window in White's. We watched the world and I snapped it as one of those moments. Aunt Sadie liked near the window, Mam said. She watched the fashion and imagined she played a full part in the life of the city. Then she did, I said. We talked a bit about the sickness now, under the outer layer of normality. The feeling that some of the men passing by might not be just men passing by. The niggling fear that made you glance to make sure that anyone who took a parcel in, took it out with them. I had a feeling of being one of the people of this place, of this time, maimed by it all and not able to do anything about it.

Yet there was some sort of tiny mood edging in. A small uplift, that we two were lucky because of a certain amount of control, because of the strength of our family, maybe a refinement. Something that's difficult to describe. But you know, I came out of White's feeling overall secure and optimistic.

I dropped some coins into a tramp's hat. He reinforced my mood. He didn't threaten me and he was like an old building – a necessary part of the city. He suggested permanency and I admired him for having survived the turmoil of the last few years. When I looked into his weak, distant eyes I thought, maybe he hasn't noticed any difference. What are a few bangs, a photo in the paper, and some extra rubble in the life of a man who has no one to mourn and whose bed is the grey brick of a doorway?

Big thoughts.

We did some shopping in the British Home Stores. Underwear for me, slippers for Dad.

She doesn't show her emotions easily. Neither do I. But I think we both knew. I had that feeling coming back in the taxi. You know, easy.

Wednesday 0050 hours

I'm in about a half an hour. Mimi Roberts was at the door and she called me over. Do you know how much your mother worries about you? she asked me. I'm worried about her, I said. Have you noticed how often she cleans those cups? Never mind the cups, Mimi said. Do you know the sort that's in the city these days? She's worried you're mixed up in something. The last thing I am, I said to Mimi, is mixed up. I had to keep it light. But she went on, She's worried sick. Why don't you stay in at night? Just until this is all over. You're all she's got, you know. I'm alright, I said, don't you worry about me. It's only a game. What's a game, she asked me. Billiards, I said. I declare to God, she said, and shut the door. I stood a minute looking at the dark green door and I could see old Mimi limping back into the kitchen. But what could I say to her? What can you say to Mimi Roberts?

Anyway, Ma wasn't bad when I came in. She still had a big fire and music on the radio. Mimi was at the door, I told her, for something to say. I had a word with her. She was looking at the stars. A fat lot of stars she can see between them roofs, Ma said. I boiled the kettle and she took a drink of tea. She started telling me again about the time the three of us stayed in Newcastle for our holidays and they took me down to the beach at night to see the moon on the sea. It was like a picture, she said. There wasn't a breath, and to top it all we heard music in the distance.

I came on up here. About earlier on – I hung around outside the dole till some of the office workers came out. I watched from across the street. Then she came, but she was with another girl. They were laughing. She was wearing a blue trench coat with a belt. I followed them down the street. The other girl was chattering away, but she was listening mostly. She has class, and the odd time she shook her hair back over her shoulders. They parted at the corner. I stood and watched her walking on up towards the city centre. Just watched her and thought of her standing in the shadow of her room, near the window with the curtains open, quietly taking off her clothes and letting them drop on the carpet. I couldn't have interrupted that. Not then.

Gerry called tonight with Sam's orders to go and meet some people in Nutcracker's Suite. Gerry remarked to me that Sam's keeping a low profile these days. The more important you get, I said. A couple of big names talked to us about the future, the way it's going to go, how much we are needed. This type of thing. We're getting closer, Gerry said on the way home.

Wednesday afternoon 12.30

Chuck says, how can you compare a life with an idea. You can't kill one person to achieve something, not even one. You haven't the right, it just isn't yours. Pete argued about extreme frustration, but Chuck said, even that. There are more effective ways anyway, ways that would unite people. Killing only divides them more. Because killing is the ultimate fear.

Dad is sporting his new slippers and he came up with a good idea. What about a dart board, Sarah, he said. To keep the boys going. And myself and Chuck might even join in. We might even make it into a club if it's successful. Mam smiled at him as if he was a child and he sat down at the fire with his folded paper on his knee, looking into the flames and seeing his dart board and all the lads around it. And maybe something from his past. I know he's thinking about our Barney as well because the Principal says he needs careful watching. He feels he has a grievance and he could be perfect bait. They've agreed to let up on the homework to try to take the pressure off. It's only right. School should be a haven for children these days. To keep them from escaping into the arms of something worse.

School should be happy. A place for unworry. Because boys and girls aren't sure. Tasting, touching, sampling, waiting. And letting it be.

Matt and I walked and talked last night. And planned. We went through it all again so there won't be any hitches. Sailing out and away. Away from what? All this, all of it crowding behind and us separating away, drifting out in a dark water cloud. Swaying on top of it like the waves we used to draw on the page in school. The squiggly waves with the ship sailing above. Always across the horizon. Never coming back. Never really.

Wednesday 2350 hours

Just back from Vera's. Went to check Sam's whereabouts. She was on her own. I'm waiting for him too, she said. Sam's an elusive hawk, she said. The royal blue dressing gown was belted. I said I didn't mean to interrupt, I'd head on if Sam's not here. After all, he could be at my house. Come in, she said, the coffee's on. If there's one thing about this house, she said when she was going into the kitchen, it's that the coffee's always on. And the dressing gown, I thought.

I couldn't imagine Vera with relatives, or a job or anything. She's just Vera.

Where did you meet Sam, I asked her, when we were sitting drinking our coffee. The record player was on low, the man's voice was scraping. It was thin, sort of like an echo I heard one time in a cave. Matt Munroe's great, she had said when she was dusting the record with the sleeve of her dressing gown. Great, I said. I always agree when it's not worth disagreeing. I was beginning to think that on Vera's turntable everybody sounded the same. Reduced to the same small squeak. Maybe Sam would buy her a new one some day.

It wasn't a case of meeting Sam, she said. He just sort of arrived, or maybe he was always here. I seem to forget, she laughed. She was sitting on the couch with her legs up under her. One bare knee was sticking out. There were goose pimples on it, or maybe it was her age. But it had a mystery I would have liked to explore. Sam knew it. Even it was Sam looking out at me.

To get off the subject of Sam, in case it got to him that I was making enquiries, I told her I had met a nice girl. Oh really, she said and leant towards me. Now you tell me, 'cause I'd really like to know, what's a nice girl? It embarrassed me. Well, it's not something you can describe. You just know.

It was getting late and the cup was empty.

I'll tell Sam you called, Vera said. It was just in case I was needed, I said. Of course, Vera said.

Women like Vera are to be taken with a pinch of salt. She makes you feel like Matt Munroe sounds on her record player. But who is she, anyway? Who is Vera?

Ma's still padding about the room. What does she be doing? Drawers opening, scrawling closed, things thudding on the floor. Sometimes I think it's her, but I hear the noises again and her breath. She breathes heavy these days. I wait for the click of the light switch and the springs of the bed. Then silence.

Thursday evening 7.40

Another day to go. Most of my stuff is packed. Me and Sadie went through it all. You've enough there for two weeks, Sadie said. It's hard to judge, I told her. She's lending me her good coat with the felt collar.

Our Pete's looking at me like a sorry pet dog I'm leaving behind. I never thought of it that way but maybe with me and him not working, he thought we were, well, the same. He's watching me from a corner, a dark corner with the light shining away from it. You know the feeling on a sunny day when the sun suddenly vanishes and dullness takes over. I feel like that when I look at him. He's making me feel guilty. He's making me sink. At least our Madge moans openly, never leaves you in any doubt about how she's feeling. She spits it all out before it gets near the depths. Our Pete's a sad soaker, a sad soaker without an outlet. Like a black hole in the sand when the tide comes in and gradually it fills up. It's bound to overflow.

Our Pete is the black hole.

Dad came into the room a minute ago. He gave me twenty pounds. I told him about the diary. He said that's good, that's very good. I thought he was going to say something else but he didn't seem to think of anything. When he left I wondered did he feel out of place now with us all growing up and him not coming in on a Friday with his pay or anything. He always shaves and dresses well. At first he used to say, in case somebody calls from the dole. To show I'm ready for a job. But nobody ever called and he just kept up the habit. Dad believes in an even life. Keep on the smooth surface, no matter who around is rising or falling.

Private thoughts for England. To keep me company. To remind me and maybe deepen the experience or detach me from it. If I want that.

Friday 1420 hours if the clock's right

I wish I had a longer name. She smiled. Warmer than for the man in front. I drank her perfume and it tingled through my body. I can still smell it. Maybe it passed onto my clothes. My hand nearly touched hers when she reached to take the card. It nearly did, and we looked straight into each other's eyes so that we were telling each other. I swear we were. Hers are round and almost green. In a dark entry they would shine and melt in sorrow. It would be like a close-up in a film. I would make her cry just to watch her tears and to protect her. And then she would sleep with her hair falling all over the white pillow and she would know that I was there, so that a silent peace would rest on her lips. I love her. She knows my name.

Time out in Birmingham

It began when they were met at the station. She stepped inside the person who was waiting on the platform.

Matthew's brother was also waiting with a broad smile and a look of possession on his face. He could have been standing at the entrance to a large country house. He could have been saying, 'I bought this with my own money. Welcome.' He did say 'Welcome'. Colette smiled shyly and gratefully.

'This is Colette,' Matthew said.

Colette peeled herself from the memory of the crossing and held her hand out to the stranger grinning self-assuredly before her.

'This is Christopher,' Matthew said.

'Christopher,' she repeated, 'Good to see you.'

'And a pleasure to meet you.' Christopher bowed slightly towards her.

Matthew looked from one to the other. Proudly. 'Right,' he said, 'Are we right?'

Colette walked between them out of the station. She was distantly present, relieved at the refinement of the people around. They were having polite conversations, in twos and in groups and weren't spitting and swearing and sliding in pools of Guinness.

'How was the crossing?' Christopher asked.

'Dreadful,' Matthew said.

'They always are,' Christopher commented. 'On account of the peasants.' He laughed.

Colette stepped into the car. She sat in the back behind the two brothers and looked from side to side as they drove through the streets of Birmingham. In order not to miss anything, not to miss Birmingham. To encapsulate it, store it.

'Lin will have a nice lunch prepared,' Christopher inclined his head towards her. 'Chinese style. I hope you'll like it.'

'We've eaten Chinese food,' Mathew said casually.

Christopher laughed. 'In the restaurants you mean? Oh please, don't say that to Lin. Oh no, that wouldn't do.'

Matthew looked at his brother in slight confusion.

'I'm sure we'll love it,' Colette said, demurely.

She was relieved that she hadn't been the one to mention the Chinese restaurants. Exercising caution often paid off. Maintaining silence could be interpreted in many ways, ignorance being only one of them, but making an outright blunder – well, that was unambiguous to say the least.

Christopher pointed out various places of interest along the way. Colette listened but asked no questions.

There were people from various parts of the world here. Apart from the coloured soldiers who moved in sunlight and shadows close to garden walls, and of course, (dare she mention it even to herself?) the men and women who served in the Chinese restaurants, and their attractive children, all the people she had ever known wore the same pinky, whitey skin, with slight variations of red and even purple. But nothing like this. She was surprised that she had to admit to a feeling almost approaching fear, or was it simply strangeness.

She was struck by the volume of traffic and the scale of the movement of people. There appeared to be more hurry than in Belfast. She remembered the unemployment situation but considered that, nevertheless, the people she saw through the window had somewhere to go. She also had somewhere to go. She and Matthew had travelled across the Irish Sea. They had chosen to do so and here they were being driven through the streets of Birmingham. It was movement. It was choice and, more than these, it was like a flower of possibility opening up its petals.

'Of course we'll have a closer look at the centre of Birmingham,' Christopher was saying. 'Maybe this afternoon if you're up to it. A weekend isn't very long but we have a few things lined up.'

'We might never go back,' Matthew smiled round at Colette. She looked confidently happy in the shadow of the back seat.

'Anything's possible,' she said. But then, not to give the wrong impression, not to worry Christopher with the thought that, secretly, they might be planning to plant themselves on him, she added, 'If only we had no commitments.'

'Indeed, commitments,' Matthew agreed.

'Well, let's forget about those for the weekend,' Christopher said.

'This is Smethwyck now,' he told them as they drove down a road with no special features. He looked at his watch. 'We're fairly well on time. Lin likes punctuality.'

This extension to the previously uncomplicated portrait of Lin, the Chinese girl, caused Colette's thoughts to jolt. It was definite and demanding, to like punctuality. She considered what it implied and wondered what could be said of her – 'Colette likes – ?'

'Yes, I'm pretty keen on being on time myself,' Matthew said. He was straightening his tie. 'Isn't that right, Colette?'

The houses and people moved back in a bleary way, out of her gaze. She continued staring through the side window but somehow Lin stood there. Waiting. An uneasy thought buzzed in her mind. What was it Matthew was saying about punctuality? But Christopher saved her from having to respond. He turned to his brother.

'What, you?' he said derisively. 'That's something new if you do.'

'What do you mean?' Matthew accosted him.

'I seem to remember that you held the school record for late marks,' Christopher answered.

'What's that got to do with it?' Matthew said. He laughed and his brother joined in. Colette laughed. She noted how similar the backs of their heads were, and tried to picture them running, schoolbags slung into the school yard. She heard children's voices of abandon in the past.

The car stopped. They were outside a three-storeyed

terraced house in a long street of three-storeyed terraced houses.

'This is it,' Christopher announced.

There was nothing to say. No need to comment on the fact that this was it. Matthew stretched, yawned and, as his brother got out of the car and went to the boot, he turned and looked at Colette.

'Are you alright?' he asked, reaching his hand in and touching hers.

'Yes, I'm really fine,' she answered. She smiled.

'You've been strange since we met Christopher,' he said.

'How?' she asked and inclined her head a little to the side.

'I don't know,' he hesitated. 'Just strange.'

'I'm not used to meeting people,' she said unconvincingly.

But she was pleased because it meant that Matthew had noticed she was different.

'Come on, you two, I'm not carrying all this myself,' Christopher shouted in at them.

'Coming,' Matthew said.

'He has a slight Birmingham accent,' Colette said when they were climbing from the car. Christopher was at the front door.

'Well, here goes,' Matthew straightened himself and dusted his jacket.

'Lin is waiting,' Colette whispered.

'Hi, darling.' Lin smiled over Christopher's shoulder, out of his embrace, regarding the newcomers from the security of her world. Colette was struck by a mysterious beauty in her face. It was mysterious yet open. Both these qualities merged and Colette found herself having to reconsider. Start again. Because this was Lin. That was the point.

Colette stood apart from Matthew. She could not have smiled out of his embrace. Not publicly. But it wasn't only that. The smile she returned, though genuine, was not out of a world. It was out of uncertainty. It was on the edge of a background that at this moment shimmered and shook and threatened to crumble and fall away.

'You're welcome,' Lin said. She came forward and took each of their hands in turn. 'We will try to make your stay enjoyable.' Her English was impeccable and attractively spoken.

'Thank you,' Colette said.

'Everything here is wonderful,' Colette thought. She accepted a second glass of wine and said aloud, 'Everything here is wonderful.' Was it giving too much away? In other words, if everything here was so wonderful, what was she used to? So far all she had done was have a Chinese lunch, delicious though it was, and one glass of wine. But they were all smiling and she had spoken out confidently. Matthew was puffing on a large cigar and, in the slight haze which had developed, it appeared to Colette that nothing suited Matthew better than to puff on a large cigar. Another way of looking at it was that the cigar was in control and was commanding clouds of smoke to emanate from Matthew's mouth at irregular intervals.

It was relaxing. Christopher insisted on showing his brother the many cupboards, units, drawers and wooden things with no names which he had made to adorn the flat. Matthew asked questions about how they were assembled.

Colette watched Lin's face discreetly and saw the Oriental darkness of her past and the bright fulfilment of her present. She helped her to clear the lunch things away but she felt clumsy in the kitchen and a little light. She made the excuse that she was tired after the journey and came back to the room to finish her glass of wine. She smiled broadly and thought the afternoon would wave comfortably in front of her. And that she would talk presently.

Lin curled up on the couch. She had her shoes off and her head was resting on Christopher's shoulder. It upset Colette who thought, we don't do things like that in Belfast. Not in front of people. Besides, it's difficult to converse with people who are stuck together. Whose brains are interwoven.

'I'd like to unpack please,' Colette said. She glanced towards Matthew who smiled as though to say, go ahead.

Lin sprang up. 'Of course,' she said. 'I shall take you to your room.'

Your room. In the plural. She sat on the bed and thought about that. It was so natural. Like 'our room'. This is our room. But it was so stupid the way she had blushed and looked confused. Because there was no answer to that. Yet it was pleasant. It was wavering in front of her like she had expected.

She began unpacking. There was a chest of drawers each. How does one achieve this, she thought. She sat on the bed and laughed at the idea of it all. She laughed at the two chests of drawers, tidied out and prepared, with clean brown paper lining each drawer. She laughed at the dressing table with its white lace mats. At the empty wardrobe with hangers waiting. At the fresh pink bedspread and the clean white pillows.

She laughed and became serious in anticipation of the stranger who would enter the room. They were all strangers down there. All together and strangers, and across the blue depths, the sinking, moving, gathering waters of separation there was the family. She had been peeled off. Was it too much to ask, that she could act separately, whole? She got up and stood at the window. Looking across the stark, still rooftops and, all the way the buildings pushed into the skyline, all the way, with the many people of a city huddled underneath. Was it any different? But it was, because of the Oriental girl downstairs and Matthew's brother who had made all the cupboards, and their lives together. And the fact that she was up here alone looking out at unfamiliarity.,

It was the thin shaft of light that woke her, that caused her thoughts to climb and wander through amazement and doubt and shivery secret knowledge. He was there, sleeping intimately. They hadn't discussed it but she had been preoccupied for the rest of the day. As though she had made a statement about herself. To him. To them. And yet what had she done other than to accept the room?

It was being taken for what she maybe wasn't. Publicly.

Privately, his whole skin was surprisingly babyish. They fitted in warm shapes and she had the same doubts and joys about their intimacies. The intimacies of those who aren't quite ready. It was no different, sleeping together, except the long closeness. Matthew hinted at a sophistication but was calmed and ultimately satisfied. Enough to grunt and snuggle into her silence. It was alright, but the yellow line of light persisted and unsettled her and in the end it was the knowledge of the couple lying in the next room, enwrapped in complacency, which disturbed her rest.

So that Matthew awoke to find her sitting at the bottom of the bed, fiddling with her nightdress ribbons.

'Colette?'

She moved to the window and parted the curtains slightly. A weak morning light sprinkled across the bedclothes. She closed the curtains and moved over to the wardrobe.

'I'm getting up,' she said.

Matthew poked for his watch. 'It's only a quarter past seven,' he mumbled.

'Is it?'

'Come on back to bed.'

What was there to do at a quarter past seven? In the house of strangers in an unfamiliar city? What was there to do that they would notice, become aware of?

'I'm too quiet,' she said. She was lying staring upward and Matthew was on his side watching her. He laughed affectionately and moved closer.

'How do you make that out?' He kissed the side of her face.

'No,' she said. She wriggled further to the edge of the bed. 'I mean I'm too quiet. I am.'

They walked amongst busy market stalls and foreign coloured fabrics. Rising, chattering, singing accents, broken and unbroken, speckled the confused air, the crowded picture sucking them forward, spurting them backwards. Colette wandered in the force. On her own she could have wandered tastefully, still with the taunting vision, alone, experiencing. But Lin's pace scorned hesitation, darting playfully, she knew where she was going, what she wanted. And even if she didn't, there was knowledge in that. It was her manner. Lifting materials gracefully and expertly, her deft handling unaffected by scrutiny. 'What do you think of this, Colette? For the bathroom window.' 'Very nice. It would do well.' Rejected, dropped into the shocking pile, swallowed back by the heaving patchwork cloth monster. It was horrible in the first place. But she had been asked and she wanted to be right. It was stupid, she had been unprepared, unthinking. She trailed and she was being denied the experience.

The brothers were in a nearby bar, together, where she would have liked to have been, sharing, talking. Why had he assumed she would wish to shop. A woman likes to shop even if she's buying nothing. Women together, he would expect them to come back with a developed togetherness. He would see her alienation, her slumped quietness. He would see Lin's radiant satisfaction, her plastic bag of success, the fresh fish, her bargaining power written all over the loose vegetables, the specialist spices. The ingredients of a well-planned meal. An ordered half of a solid relationship, a carved corner protected by sureness. He would see her empy arms beside, her sullen attitude, because she felt it. And it wasn't that she wanted to be like Lin. It was that she didn't know.

'I'm tied up,' she said. 'I've a feeling I might never get free.'

'Free from what?' Matthew asked her, but he didn't want a long discussion. He was tired of discussions about freedom and oppression and downtrodden people. He was enjoying this, immediately enjoying it and planning in his brain that it would be his. And hers. He wanted her to snap out of it.

'You seemed so confident on the way here in the car.'

'I was.'

'Are you worried about them at home?'

'Who?'

'Your family.'

'I don't think so. Not worried.'

'Then what?'

'I might have to go off on my own.'

'Why?'

'Because I might not be capable of it. I might not.'

'They seem very happy, don't they?' He nodded towards the other room.

'Seem. But it's superficial.' She had to say that. And she had to say, 'If you want that with me you'll never have it. It's neat. You know what I mean, neat. Neat and nothing.'

Matthew spent some time over his preparations.

'We never do things like this at home,' he said. He was combing his hair above her, into the dressing-table mirror, perfecting its shape, parting the smooth thickness and finally leaving it to rest like a carefully placed cap.

Colette glanced up. She had a smudge of beige foundation liquid unspread on her cheek.

'You've a fine head of hair,' she said.

'Do you like it?' He patted it, pleased.

'It's healthy,' she said.

They would look good together. It was good to look good together. She was at ease when they stepped into the car. Eating out represented equality. Eating together, drinking wine, and talking. It was an even, undemanding thing to do.

She suggested a lot. A lot behind, before, after. And mysterious pauses. Lin did not understand, clearly could not fathom the loops and folds, the profundities. Matthew supported, denied, stated that it was all dreadful, strangling, but could be sorted out or left. He would leave it, they would leave it.

'I have left it,' Christopher said. He turned his soul to Lin who spread herself into a smile and cut them out momentarily with a kiss.

'Just right, and I will too,' Matthew said. 'We will, won't we Colette? It's her large family, coming from a large family.'

'Oh, yes, I would love a large family,' Lin said. 'In fact I shall have a large family.'

'It's to be with, yet alone,' Colette said, leaning forward as though that were it, the final word. She raised her wine glass and smiled at Matthew who sat back relaxed, and sipping.

'It's been good but it's nearly over,' Matthew said.

'I spoke to a coloured man,' Colette said. She was drinking tea and kneeling flipping over Christopher's LPs.

'It's a bit much, all the same, them taking off like that at this time of the evening. I mean with us here as guests and all.'

'It's been a tiring weekend for them. They need a rest.' She examined the cover of one of the records, accentuating her detachment.

'Some rest,' Matthew sulked.

She got up and came towards him, with the record swinging teasingly in her hand. 'I tell you what,' she said, 'We'll go up ourselves for half an hour.'

A bright suspicion flickered in Mathew's eyes.

'Go on, you go on up, I'll follow you when I rinse these cups.' She nudged him encouragingly and affected an innocent cuteness by lowering her head and widening her eyes.

Matthew went to rise, then changed his mind. 'You're having me on,' he said.

'Am I? Oh, alright then, we'll forget it. Forget I ever said it.' She got up and went towards the kitchen.

'No, listen, I'm away up. I'll expect you.' Matthew touched her shoulder, gave her a long look, then left the room.

Colette sat on the floor and listened to the music, the words, the experienced meaning of Paul Simon. It was new to her, new yet old. She wondered had Matthew fallen asleep or was he seething.

Finally the voice irritated her, the message, line after line, the air to make it attractive, the message or the meaning, the song after song, and the threat that there was another side. It was an interference after all.

She went upstairs. Matthew was pulling on a jacket. He scarcely glanced when she closed the door behind her.

'Are you going somewhere?' she asked.

'I'm going to the pub. I'll be back for dinner.' He opened the door.

'No, wait,' she said, 'I might as well . . .'

'Might as well what?'

'Go too,' she said.

'I'll see you,' he said.

'I'm going out,' she shouted after him. 'I'm going out. I'm not sitting here for the next hour and a half.' But he was gone. And they probably heard her, through one wall they were bound to, and it would sound awful to hear her shouting that, that she couldn't spend the next hour and a half sitting here. It was ungrateful to say the least. She would be embarrassed at dinner and maybe that was what mattered, that she would be embarrassed.

They were furrowing in a huge blob of rippling ink. The drone of the boat sliced through the dark blue desert, cutting it and leaving it intact. Behind, it sprayed and settled, met and bobbed, and the increasing mass of rolling liquid shimmered permanently.

'We're nowhere,' Colette said.

'You're never nowhere,' Matthew said. They were looking into it, across it. Colette had her collar up against the cold and her hair blew wildly. He was holding onto her, as if afraid she might be sucked into the black force of air and water.

'It's the nearest thing to nowhere,' she said. If you thought of nowhere you thought of darkness, a sort of falling black. Like death. Was it because when you closed your eyes you saw black, or because the night brought darkness. Those who believed in an afterlife thought of light, light glowing radiantly, everywhere. Those who didn't believe saw themselves sinking into dark permanent nothingness. Some could cope with that.

'Oh God, I forgot to ask for Pete,' she said.

'Ask what for Pete?' When he spoke he was receiving comfort from her nearness. She felt that and it sparked a thin flame of regret that she hadn't made more of it, that they had had all that time together and, in a way, she had been foraging into its possibilities, irritably shutting off little openings, nipping buds. Standing between herself.

'For a job. I told Pete.'

'It's freezing up here,' he said. 'Come on down we'll have a cup of tea.'

They sat opposite each other. She warmed her hands on the cup and felt the coldness drain from her face.

'There's nobody to ask,' he said.

'What?' She was smoothing her hair down now and thinking she wanted to lie in the warm shape. Now that she couldn't. Nobody would take away what they had known, yet they could lose it themselves.

'There's nobody to ask for Pete,' he said.

'I wish I could say I tried,' she said. 'At least that would be something.'

Bangor for the day

Fragmented thoughts of her. There was a lot he didn't understand – the people who stood in the four corners of his mind. His mother, Sam, Vera, and her. They were in his mind, so he possessed them, their experience of him. He told of it in the diary and of his growing importance, the swaying reality of his fringe involvement.

When he was a boy they used to take to the mountain occasionally. They always seemed to be looking for the path. Everybody uses it, they would say, it must be here somewhere. Maybe it's overgrown, they said. When they found a path they climbed ecstatically, only to find often that it led nowhere, but faded into the general growth. His mother would say, 'I couldn't have gone any further anyway. It's time to rest.' And she would plant herself on a stone and point out to him the city below. He would drink water from the big lemonade bottle. It was as if they had reached the summit.

You were always working on hints. It was a question of interpretation, acting on a look, a word that to someone else could appear meaningless. It was to be on the uptake, to accept messages. He knew. It was why they needed him.

Sam had called and was gone, but the point was not that he was gone, but that he had called. There were instructions, passed on by his mother who thought they were all to do with the game of billiards. Or in letter form. Places mentioned, meetings taking place, doors opening onto other doors which sometimes seemed to shut just as he reached them, whereupon he reinterpreted the original message or accepted the test patiently.

Protection was a word he understood. It referred to people, to territory, to ideas. To be the protector, not the aggressor was to be on the side of right. He accepted his role. It had been given to him, but in a sense it had always been his. There were examples from his schooldays, so that it would be said later it was always obvious he would stand out. Leaders had a certain look too, a look that suggested their experience of the deeper aspects of life, a look that was lacking on the face of any businessman he had seen in the newspaper. Or any politician, for that matter. He had that look. He could see it in the mirror. It was there alright.

It was some vague thought or maybe a dream in the early morning, that hazy floating period when the eyes refuse to recognise the return of the conscious state, and thoughts and dreams overlap, that set the plan in motion. When he got up it became clearer and stronger, it became a message. It was to go to Bangor, to wander around Bangor because that's where he would take her on their first date. Out of the city and down to Bangor. In the train. Bangor had class and it had anonymity. He wondered had Vera ever been to Bangor. Had she ever been out of her flat, when it came to it. Not that it mattered. Not that it mattered what Vera did, except in so far as she was a part of Sam's world.

'I'm going on a bit of a trip today,' he told his mother. He was eating the juicy buttered baps she had set before him, the fresh buttered baps she ran out to get every morning for his breakfast. Behind him the morning fire blazed. He never came down to a cold grate. She was slithering between the table and the fire, tending to both, but when she heard his threat she stood before him, rubbing her hands on the front of her apron.

'A trip?' she repeated.

'Down to Bangor,' he said, ignoring her alarm and continuing to stuff the fresh dough into his mouth, following each mouthful with a gulp of tea.

'I'm going to Bangor for the day. It's a treat. I'm treating myself to a day in Bangor.'

She was concerned to establish that he was going alone, and when she was reassured that he was friendless, she sat down at the corner of the fire.

'Mimi's calling on her way from the shops,' she said.

When he was setting off down the hall she called after him to mind the water.

Along the street he met Mimi, straining to one side to balance the black, bulging shopping bag which burdened her other arm.

'I'm going to Bangor for the day,' he told her. He walked on before she had time to react.

There was destiny in the reflection in the train window. Beyond and through it fields and trees fled. It was amazing what could be accomplished; he saw the flame that never went out. It burned there, constantly threatened, often almost extinguished, but it came back before it had gone. It never went. Damn, he'd forgotten to leave a message for Sam. What if today was to be a big day? You would never know until it arrived. What if he missed it? Gone to Bangor for the day. How would that sound? He felt an itchy heat rising inside his clothes, causing him to shift about in his seat. He knew he was blushing and that the woman opposite would notice him. She had failed to be impressed by his equanimity. In fact she had not raised her eyes from the book she was reading. But she would become aware of him now. He was willing her to look, despite himself.

He rose suddenly and let down the window, offering his face to the disturbed air, letting it cool and bathe him rapidly. And then it occurred to him. He would ring Vera, leaving a message for Sam, gauging from her reaction whether he was needed. Because she mightn't say anything direct. He wouldn't expect her to say anything direct.

He closed the window and resumed his seat. Taking his comb

from his top pocket, he rearranged his hair and turned to look into himself in the window again. The woman shuddered slightly, feeling the sharpness of the cold air and sent a disapproving glance his way. Then she went back to her fictitious world.

'Vera? Have you seen Sam today?'

'Sam? No, not today.'

'How are things, Vera?'

'Things? Alright. Everything's alright.'

'In the city – I mean is everything – em, under control?'

'What are you talking about?'

'Nothing, Vera, nothing, I'm probably just a bit – homesick.'

'Homesick? Look, where are you?'

'Me? In Bangor.'

'Bangor?' Vera's scornful laugh rang in his ear but he managed to convey his message in an even, controlled voice.

'If Sam rings, tell him I checked in. Goodbye, Vera.'

He put the receiver down and left the phone box. As he walked down the main street he considered the fact that Vera could be a spanner in the works. With a woman like Vera you were never quite sure. She could know everything or she could know nothing.

When he reached the bottom of the hill he turned and began to walk back up again, this time with his head raised and his eyes alert. For interesting places to bring her.

A couple of elderly people sat in the shelter, huddling against the sea wind. The old woman had a tartan blanket over her knees. They stared beyond, drawing separate lines with their eyes, out to the chopping white frills which adorned the expansive waste of flouncing green silk. They could have been seeing the hacked wasteland of their lives, or their gaze might have been one of resignation, that after all it had come to this. Slow days of watching and waiting, knowing there was nothing more to do, but watch the endless, changing motion of the sea. Accepting the reassurance of its moving beauty. Their look could have been one of peace. They may have turned and smiled serenely at one another when he passed.

He did not know what they were doing there. Maybe they

were out of a home and were put down there every day for the good of their health. Maybe they were waiting to be brought back, thinking of a warm fire and their dinner. Perhaps they complained bitterly every day, old people did complain a lot, but could do nothing about it. And it wasn't the warmest day to be sitting in an open shelter with the sea air blasting in at you. The old man's nose was blue.

He turned across the hard, wet sand, pressing the soggy, grey-brown wrinkles with his shoes. It was as if he was going to meet her at the edge.

And there she was, a distant figure but it was clearly her. At first, as he approached her, she grew no closer. He was tramping along the meeting place of land and water so that the shallow, spreading water squelched under his feet. He could feel it seeping through a hole in the sole of his shoe, sending a cool dampness into his sock, gradually moistening the skin on his foot. He tried walking on the side of his foot to lessen the discomfort but that was worse, so he decided to pretend it wasn't there.

At first she didn't see him coming. She was facing outward, paddling in water up to her ankles, hoisting up her skirt, even though there was no need to. She was holding her face towards the salty freshness. It suited her so much more than the background of office walls and piled files, and here he was, a lone, dark, walking figure with a fixed, serious gaze. He had stepped from the queue of names as she knew he must. She turned towards him, shyly at first and then ran, spraying water from each foot in turn, and they were laughing and holding each other in a wilderness where only they mattered.

He saw the figures of the old people labouring towards the steps and then, looking around, he realised he had the whole beach to himself. He wished they hadn't left because he felt an intense loneliness now. He remembered a similar feeling before. It was on a sunny day during the school holidays when he ran out onto the street, full of expectancy, and there was no-one there.

On the way home in the train he thought he might call in to see Vera. But there was something about the way Vera treated you. He was afraid he might break down and tell her that underneath it all he was alone, that he would cry into the deep crevice between her big, soft breasts. And that she would rock him and maybe after a while take him in to her bed.

If it hadn't been for Sam he might have done that.

'There's a lot of old people in Bangor,' he told his mother. She was fussing over him, especially after he'd mentioned the hole in his shoe. He had his bare foot up at the fire and she had the shoes out in the hall to remind her to bring them to the mender's the next morning.

'They go down to the seaside to end their days,' she said. 'But I don't know. I'd rather die near me own.'

'They spend the day looking at the sea,' he said. 'There were two doing it today. Just staring out there.'

'Mimi Roberts is coming over to hear all about it,' his mother said.

Gerry expressed dissatisfaction. He was impatient with the set-up. The initial excitement of involvement was over and it seemed to be dragging on, with nothing happening.

'We're not doing anything,' he said. 'If you ask me, we're being left out.'

'We're preparing,' Joe told him. 'You can't just walk in at the top. Everybody has to be sure of you.'

'I'm beginning to think there is no top to this,' Gerry persisted. He had his forlorn face resting on the palm of his hand, his elbow on the table.

'Wise up,' Joe said. Gerry's dismal expression irritated him. 'Where do you think Sam is? If there's no top?'

'I don't know. You tell me.' Gerry livened up, took his arm down and looked angrily at Joe, as if this was the point he was trying to make.

'If you ask me, he's giving us the shove,' he said.

'Important people can't be around,' Joe said.

'Important people,' Gerry echoed. 'What proof have we that Sam's important. You give me one example –'

Joe rose from his seat. 'Shut up. Gerry,' he said, trying hard to control his voice. 'You'd better watch what you say. You're annoying me now, and you're saying too much.'

As he turned to go he said, 'You know you're ruining your chances of getting anywhere. Don't say I didn't warn you.'

Sam had left a message. He felt like racing back and showing Gerry the proof. 'Meet at Cronies cove. Tomorrow night 10.30.' Just that.

'Did Sam leave it himself?' he asked his mother. He was looking at the words again and feeling a surge of importance and excitement.

'Didn't I tell you he did?' she said. She was craning her head round his shoulder, trying to read it. 'What does it say?' she asked.

'Say? An important message – a game,' he said. 'I'm in the finals.'

'Wouldn't you know yourself if you were in the finals?'

He was taken aback by her apparent comprehensive knowledge of the game.

'Well, no, not exactly,' he said. 'They had to toss for it in the end.'

'What did you pick?'

'Heads.'

He was away running up the stairs, crazy to get drinking in the words again because, although he hadn't admitted it at the time, Gerry's mood had disturbed his confidence. But it was Gerry who was the unfortunate one because his problem was that he'd no faith.

As soon as he had gathered himself he came down for his supper.

'Is there no music on?' he asked his mother.

'Do you want some?' She hurried over to the radio and began journeying through the stations.

'Now, is that alright?'

It sounded like jazz to him but it wasn't bad at all.

'Aye, that's okay,' he said. 'Here, Ma, would you give us a bit of a haircut in a minute?'

She got up straight away.

'My God, you don't have to jump up as if the house was on fire,' he said as she passed him like a bolt into the scullery.

'I want to find them sharp scissors,' she said. He heard her rummaging in the drawer and then she came in, smoothing the bright silver on her skirt. 'I always keep them in that drawer,' she said.

'Then you didn't have to find them,' he said. He turned in his chair and faced her.

'What do you mean?' She sat at the fire, continuously rubbing the silver on the check fabric of her skirt, and giving him a cautious stare.

'If you knew where they were.'

'You're in a funny mood,' she said, with a hint of a smile.

A shade had settled over the estate now. Colours were dulled by thoughts of away. Looking down from her bedroom, the drab houses squatted in lowering lines, making descending patterns into the city. The alien noises of children, their commonness, their accents and loudness grated on her ears. She resented their infringement, and even her family crowded her privacy, leaving little outlet for indulgence in memory. They were all so close, buzzing in and out of rooms, forever talking. What had been hinted to her before was now blasting in her ears, the constant presence, the lack of respect. It was all the same – herself, Sadie, Madge, Pete, the rest, even her mother and father. No-one stood out. And from house to house unimportant people lived unimportant lives, and around the city unimportant people were killing equally unimportant people. Did they not realise it was all so trivial? It was all so insular and self-defeating? There was no growth, no outward, magnanimous gesture of living. They were like little sparrows chirping around and picking at each other to get at a few paltry crumbs, unable to see the open sky above them.

They weren't flying to where the reward was worth the effort. It seemed to her that she had flapped her wings and had sensed that there were pastures where the grass was not swamped. It was anywhere, but it was not here. Not here where it was swamped with tears over country, territory, crown, religion, flags. She thought of the little voices twittering each other down on the television every night and that they didn't realise it had nothing to do with her. Nothing at all.

'Did you see that?' Her father eased his darts from the board and looked around the company proudly.

'One hundred and twenty. I'm getting better every day,' he said.

The younger children sat on the table at the back of the room and clapped, while the men stood about.

Madge and Colette watched from armchairs. Madge was flinging herself up and down with elation. Colette thought she looked silly, daft to get so excited about a game of darts.

They were all in a tunnel, a tunnel which made them appear small and distant. Like looking through the wrong end of binoculars. And they were dull. She was ashamed to admit it, but they were dull. Even Chuck's wisecracks thudded weightily so that she could only smile falsely.

Pete aimed clumsily but it was obvious from the outset that his darts would never reach the board. One hit the television and he stumbled to retrieve it.

The children laughed but there was a nervous hollowness in their laughter. Their mother, having heard the front door close, came in from the kitchen and ushered them out, saying it was well past their bedtime.

Madge sat back boldly because Madge liked a scene, at anyone's expense.

Colette watched her father's face, his controlled frustration, and Chuck had already approached Pete and was saying something like, 'Come on son, you and me'll take a wee walk'. But Pete pushed him out of the way and pointed a shaking finger towards his father.

'He's the perfect one,' he accused. 'Never did anything wrong in his life. Except bringing us into this bloody awful world of course.'

Colette was jolted out of her daydream and the scene before her was large and real, the draining colour in her father's face and the bustling figure of Chuck, his colour rising, actively trying to restrain Pete. 'Come on now lad, don't say anything you'll regret. Catch yourself on now, lad.'

Her father, a man of few words, spoke slowly, in an emotional voice. 'You know, Peter,' he said, 'We're all the same in this, all in the same boat. There's none of us has any privileges. It's up to each of us to make the best of it.'

'Boat,' Pete repeated, coming close to his father and swaying in front of him. 'Some of us should never have been in the boat in the first place.'

'You've said it,' Denny said. He had been standing back but was now over facing his brother, looking at him with disgust. 'The ones who can't cope with it should never have been in it. Now get out and leave us in peace. We're having a game of darts, in case you didn't notice. And if you can't even throw a dart straight you shouldn't be here.'

'Here, here! Man overboard!' Madge shouted. She was standing in the middle of the men now, looking from one to the other in anticipation.

Pete went to lunge at Denny but was restrained by his father and Chuck.

'Colette, would you make Peter a cup of strong coffee?' Her father turned to her without releasing his grasp on his son's arm. He had never struck her as a physical man but he was tall and well built and at this moment she saw a strength in him that she admired.

From the kitchen she heard further voices, her mother's amongst them now; and Pete's sounded more anguished than angry and then she heard what sounded like crying. Madge came dashing into the kitchen.

'Oh God, that's the limit,' she said. 'A man crying.'

Saturday afternoon 4.00

Pete's remorseful. And then he does it again. He's on a course and I don't know what will stop him.

I've applied to the Civil Service, for a job somewhere in England or Scotland. Any place will do for a start. It's the only way to find out certain things, or simply to be on my own. I know at some time I will have to be on my own. Matt is going to Birmingham. He wants me to go but understands I can't. This could be my biggest mistake. I can always come back here, but Matt . . .

He tried to get it down in the diary but he couldn't. Not yet. It was too confusing and his hands were shaking, shaking so hard he couldn't get his coat off. But then again, did he want his coat off?

There was once a boy. Or he didn't know, how could he know. His Uncle George would vouch for him. Or her, she would tell them of their plans for love. Or the two old people on the beach at Bangor, they with their long experience of life, they with their distant eyes, they would provide the alibi. He was the only figure between them and their sea. But that was the wrong day. Another day altogether.

If he could get to Vera's house. He would go down the stairs, quietly and without anyone knowing, he would be away to Vera's house. He fumbled to tighten the zip on his anorak but it was already tightened, right up to his throat. He loosened it a little and went towards his bedroom door. When he opened it he heard sounds from the kitchen, so familiar, the strains of dance music. He marvelled how she always managed to find it on some station. It was always on. And shuffling, like feet, feet dancing. Now who was she dancing with? A step on her own, perhaps, or the ghost of his father, a gaunt shadow in step. Imagine losing your dance partner and nobody ever fitting in again. No-one ever did but the music kept on. Had he told Mimi Roberts about her? About his worry? It was such a relief to know Mimi would look after her.

He was halfway down the dark staircase, hesitating because of the sounds in the kitchen and because he noticed that some of the paint on the wall was peeling and he had to pick it with his finger. It would have been easy to have put a coat of paint on the walls. So easy and soothing, and she would have brought him mugs of tea. He sat on the stairs picking the yellow paint from his nail and rubbing his finger on the wall to get rid of it.

He could have been picking blood.

He shuddered and rubbed both his hands hard on the frayed stair carpet. Frayed? It was in ribbons and it was a cold place to be sitting with the draught blowing in under that front door. It would have been easy to have put a flap down there along the bottom of the door. Most houses had a flap. Mimi Roberts certainly had a flap. Had Vera a flap? Flap, trap. The reason for not going to Vera's.

He huddled into himself there until it appeared that he was warm. Warm except for his face which felt not so much cold as empty. An empty face like the man's, the man who looked into his eyes with a grey fear that was more awesome than death itself.

It was death.

He was probably dead now.

But he didn't kill him. He had nothing to do with it. He stood up on the stairs, elated. He was innocent. He was also noble and could face his mother.

It was no ghost. He slunk in under the stair rail with a new panic in his throat for if that was not Sam's voice it was . . .

The music started up again and the sliding on the kitchen lino so that the fading flowers could be nothing more than vague pink smudges. They wouldn't stand up to Sam's scraping boots. He tried to get clear in his mind what it was he was trying to get clear. Then there was a high-pitched sound in his head and he was crawling up the stairs and back into his room. He went under the bed.

Sam was waiting for him. He had betrayed Sam.

He was a cold, hollow frame, stiff and silent under the bed crouching in the grey, fluffy dust.

He came out from under the bed and considered the fact that he was acting like a lunatic, that no-one in his right senses hid under a bed. No-one would want to harm you if you acted honourably. There was always the police, the law. In the final analysis there was always the law to protect you.

He had walked away from a murder. He had walked away. No, he had run away. He had run away and he had seen them, seen them and been one of them. They had seen him, had pointed a gun at him. His lay on the ground, emptied into the dirt.

At least the man knew. The dead man knew. He wouldn't do it.

It was who to tell. When he'd worked out who to tell, it was so plausible, his position, so right. He was right. Whoever he told would sort out the details of his freedom. His freedom from fear or guilt. If he should be thought to be guilty, which was impossible since he'd done nothing wrong.

What about the maxim 'once you're in'?

If you stayed in your bedroom for the rest of your life, or under the floorboards. That was a real possibility, yes, he remembered a report in the paper about a man who had hid under the floorboards for years. It mightn't be too bad. You could build yourself a real wee nest. You could have everything you wanted down there – compared with facing the barrel of a gun. If the man had had that choice now, would he not have delighted in every moment of every dark day? Tucked away in his self-contained haven with the reassurance of his family's life going on above him.

He thought of the man's face, his fine features rigid with terror, his hands shaking and fidgeting. He could have imagined him lighting a cigarette, steadily, comfortably, or pouring a Guinness into the side of his glass, smiling upward out of the corner of his eye at his friend. It was a black and white snapshot of someone who was dead.

He would live with the face under the floorboards. They would live together.

But he hadn't done it. He had run away. That was why he had to go under the floorboards.

Protector. Preparing. Idealism sparkling the night air. A murky corner, with a man leaving a pub with his friend. A sober man, all the worse. He probably only had a couple. Let him get this straight, the point of the operation was to take the lone man, bundle the ordinary man. In a frantic scuffle to detach him from his friend who protested vehemently then feebly when he saw the guns. Reduced to pleading nonsensically, 'Come on now lads, give him a break, not him, he's one of the best, what's it for, for Christ's sake boys, we can sort this all out together, he's not in anything you know.' He was left standing and the only reason it wasn't him was that he was further from the kerb. It was the only reason.

When he was manhandled into the car the man said back in a thin, dull voice, 'Look after them, will you Chuck?'

Gerry was right, there was no top to this, only a bottom.

Only his mother could bring the food, lift the floorboards and hand it down. He felt a warm tingle of excitement gathering in his gut, dispelling the horror, so that he blushed and was impatient to get down the stairs to make the plans because it had to be done this night.

Already he saw her face looking down at him, into his dark world. She would be like an angel with the light all around her. And she wouldn't have to worry where he was. He would be there all the time. That would be her big consolation.

Her biggest problem might be keeping it from Mimi Roberts.

All sorts of wee treats would be devised, like when he was a boy and was confined to bed with an illness. His every whim would be indulged because he was living under the floor. He might even order the odd pack of Guinness from the off-licence down the street, to help pass the long hours, pouring it slowly, sipping in its froth in long slow sucks, thinking, growing old. And then the diary. Of course, there was the diary. What new significance would the diary have now? On second thoughts, the Guinness would be a problem on account of the suspicion it would arouse. He would have to forget about the Guinness but it wasn't a major sacrifice, since he'd never drunk Guinness anyway.

Joe has gone to England for a job.

Thursday afternoon 3.40

There was a drizzle in the graveyard. It never let up and I could not find one break in the clouds. We all looked miserable, not at all brave and upstanding. If the sun had been out we could have held our heads up at least. But maybe we wouldn't. Mam was so grateful to get his body back, to bury him properly. I think she feels he's resting now.

I could write some bitter things and God knows bitter things have been said by some of us. But where's the point in recording it? And all the usual statements have been issued, but what's the use in that? People have been so kind, and that is the only flicker of hope for here. But it's not really for here, it's only for people wherever they are.

Chuck and Pete are the worst. Pete is burying himself and Chuck keeps saying he should have offered to be taken instead, because of having no wife or children. Maybe he's right.

We're stamped as victims now. We'll always be the victims of the troubles, and I thought I was before. But it was the knowledge that I could be.

We want to say things to each other about him, about how he was, but we can't. We only look and choke on thoughts and our own personal regrets. Pete won't sit in the same room as any of us. Madge had to stay in the Munroes'. She couldn't go to the funeral, she was in such a state. Her eyes are all puffed out with bawling. Most of us are sedated to deaden the hell of it.

But really I think the shock has not yet reached the centre. They say it's after, when the fuss has died down, the attention, when things are as they were before except that they no longer are and never will be.

Matt put off going for a couple of weeks. He's been great but I think his relief will be even bigger now, getting away, getting out of the pit. The pit of mourning.

Saturday 2230 hours

We managed. I'm in here now. It will all be told, how we did it, her reaction. She couldn't take it in at first. I gave her as few details as possible, not to burden her with secrets. Made it seem I just happened to be somewhere at the wrong time and, because I saw something I shouldn't, my life is in danger. She wanted me to go to the police but I persuaded her the only way in this situation is to lie low. You don't know the sort that's around these days, I told her. Isn't that what I've been telling you all along, she said. I didn't involve anyone else, Sam or anybody.

I can't work it all out myself, what I was really in, and that it all amounted to taking a man because of where he lived, because of the club he was coming out of.

I saw the details in the paper. There was a photo but I didn't need a photo.

She's not sure of me. She doesn't know what to believe, and sometimes at night I can imagine her thoughts, up there on her own at the fire, putting pieces together. She tries to put Mimi Roberts off coming over. Mimi thinks she's fretting because I'm away but she can't talk to Mimi now. How can she with me down here?

It's basic at the moment, only a torch for light, and it's pretty cramped, but we'll improve it in time. The main thing is I'm safe. We've had a few hairy moments. The first time a knock came to the door she was handing me something down. We both froze and she got all agitated, rubbing her face and muttering, Oh my God, this is it, this is it. I managed to calm her down. I told her no-one could possibly notice anything and I got her to repeat after me, Joe has gone to England for a job.

Tell Joe his friends will be looking forward to seeing him, when he comes for his holidays like, they said after she had told them. That set her off for a while, talking to herself and asking herself what was going to become of us. I had to tell her if she didn't catch herself on and practise self-control, the whole thing would be ruined. Do you want me to be caught, I said. No, she said. Then put on some music and act the way you used to, I said. Put on a cup of tea or sit at the fire.

It's not too bad. I can come up at night when the curtains are closed and sit in the kitchen, although it can be awkward when she answers me sharply, cuts me off. Then there's no point to it,

I maybe read a bit and come on down again. Down to my hole, like a giant rat.

Wednesday 1435 hours

Life goes on, one dark hole day after another. Things that worry me. 1, No money now and she's finding it very tough on her pension. 2, When she races out for my fresh baps in the morning or to do any shopping, for that matter – what if she's knocked down, if she just doesn't come back and I don't know what's happened to her – what do I do? 3, If she gets ill in the house. 4, If I get ill. It can't be healthy down here and never getting fresh air. 5, No hope of a girl.

Think a lot about the girl from the dole. It gives me a pain that I didn't let her know how I felt. Sometimes I think of it now, of sending her a letter, getting Ma to take it round, letting her know. My lover under the floor. My dreams and imagination tell me there is a future for her and me. I wake up with her beside me and go through all our meetings. It's a message. I hate that she thinks I'm in England, that I went away without saying anything. Ma had to go round and tell them. If she loves me I could trust her, I could take a chance if I could find a way of letting her know. Something to be worked out.

Ma just handed me down tea and biscuits. She hadn't much of a smile on her face. If I could get her to believe I'm right, I'm only in here because of the state of this place, not because I did anything wrong. The police would have been here, I said, if I'd done anything wrong, or the army. And maybe they will too, she said. Couldn't it take them years to get round to it. Then she added with a sly look on her face, What about that final? Did you win it? No, I said, I lost.

Thursday 1000 hours

I was woken this morning by an awful nightmare. I was walking to meet the man, we were walking towards each other, keeping walking yet never getting any closer. He had a queer smile his face and his face was white with the light of the moon. It was a country road with miles of fields on either side. I was terrified, not of the man, but of who might be hiding behind the hedges. Then, coming out of the shadows behind him, I saw men with vicious scowls on their faces. He didn't see them but just kept walking on. I shouted to warn him but he didn't hear me. He never took the smile off his face, his moon smile. I looked behind me and there were men there too, coming after me with weapons, though it wasn't clear what the weapons were. I started to run and I heard their feet running behind me. I was shouting, Help me, to him and I didn't know which way to run but it didn't matter because when I started to run I wasn't going anywhere. I couldn't move and they were coming nearer. And then he wasn't there at all. It was Sam – I woke up and my whole body was soaked with sweat.

I waited for her to come to the board, to open it up and let me see her, and the light from the kitchen. When I heard her feet on the floor I said up, Ma will you open this? She rolled back the mat and lifted the lino where we slit it. She had her coat wrapped round her and all. For God's sake Ma, never mind the baps, I said. Just a cup of strong tea. Sure doesn't he keep them over for me under the counter, she said. She was rummaging in the drawer for her purse. Anyway they'd wonder if I never showed up for them.

Doesn't he know I'm away? I asked her.

I'm not beyond liking a bap myself, she said. I'm away on.

She banged the kitchen door when I was just saying don't be long, and I heard her slippers trailing down the hall. I remembered the two sounds and then the final bang of the front door. Me lying upstairs in my bed and Da down in the kitchen, when she went over to Mimi Roberts of a night. I thought I would lie awake to hear her coming back, but I was always asleep.

The baps were lovely. It was worth it.

Friday 2100 hours

We've been doing a bit of cleaning down here and laying some mats. I think she's coming round. Last night we had a game of Ludo. She was giving me chances and hoping I wouldn't notice, like not taking two goes when she got a six, or not taking another man out. She's also gone back to the music but the most important clue was when I was closing in for the night. I suppose it's not your fault son, she said. Jesus, the door.

I'm still shaking. That was Vera. She managed to get Ma to bring her in. I've something very important to talk to you about, she said. What about, Ma said. Your son, she said. They came into the kitchen and were above me, talking. It was eerie. All Ma kept repeating was, Joe has gone to England for a job. No forwarding address yet. No, I haven't heard from him. Look, I want to help, said Vera.

What do you mean, Ma asked, all innocence.

He might think he's in trouble, Vera says.

Trouble? Ma said.

Look, he has nothing to worry about, Vera said. Absolutely nothing.

If he gets a job, Ma said.

That's another thing, Vera said. But he's a free man, he has nobody to fear.

Free man? Nobody to fear? Ma had scorn in her voice. In this place? He's gone to England for a job.

Get him to write to me, Vera said. Her voice was genuine and I could hardly breath for not knowing what to think.

Aye, I might, Ma said.

He's got the address, Vera said and then it was obvious she was leaving for I heard the door handle.

Has he indeed, Ma said.

When they were going down the hall Vera was saying, I'm a friend you know, and God knows in this place you need friends. As the front door was opening she said, He's an honest boy.

He was brought up to be, Ma said and closed the door.

The first thing I wanted to know was what was Vera wearing. I had this picture of her up there in her blue dressing gown. Ma couldn't remember the colour of her coat but said she had white high heels on with the toes worn.

I had to explain away knowing Vera. Ma kept saying, I don't like the look of that one. I couldn't argue with that but I had to explain knowing her. She's the secretary of the billiards, I said.

I'm sure I don't know, Ma said. She was poking the fire and I looked on this as a bit of a setback. Anything that made me more complicated or mysterious. It had to be all simple to win her favour back.

Look at it this way, I said to her. She knows I'm honest. She knows I did nothing wrong.

One like that one would be better off not knowing anything about you, she said.

I've been tormenting myself. Maybe Vera was my one chance. Should I have come up. But then, how can you be sure with a woman like Vera?

He'll get no job in England, Mimi Roberts said. No chance. Sure they can't give work to their own.

He's out of this place, Ma said.

Mimi was still smarting from not having been warned that I was going away. I never dreamt, she said. If you'd told me, I could have given him a wee something to help him on his way. Going off like that into the night.

He just upped and went, Ma said. It got him down.

Mimi cheered up. Sure look at it this way, she said, Maybe he'll bring home a nice wee girl.

Aye, Ma said and I heard her chair creaking. I'll make the tea, she sighed.

Mimi started humming, some old Irish air or something, and Ma was shuffling about in the kitchen. I crouched completely still in my black dugout and heard the dull sounds of cups on saucers, the teapot dumped back on the stove, the heavy top of the bread bin clanking. It was away inside me, happening, and out of my reach on the outside. It was like in the dentist's chair, under the gas, and somewhere above the depths were real sounds and voices. They were there but you couldn't get to them. Not yet. You were sinking in your own darkness. Until there was a floppy haze and you were in it. I hit the nurse on the face one time.

I'm like somebody who's just become blind. Sounds make all

the pictures. I knew when the cup left the saucer and pictured it at Ma's mouth and the red roses on the side.

There were murmurs and drolls of sentences without much connection. It went on for ages.

He's as well out of it, Mimi said.

Ma's chair creaked and after a slither on the lino there was a click and then voices and music sliced through as she searched the stations.

You couldn't have got in that door for people, she said, when she settled for a band playing something old-time.

Aye, Mimi said and I knew the looks they had in their eyes. Like the old people staring across the sea at Bangor.

Saturday 1900 hours

Fish and chips with plenty of vinegar, making greasy blobs on the outside of the brown paper. Da used to bring them in and if she hadn't the bread and butter and tea out ready on the table, he sat at the fire and started eating them out of the paper, with the steam and smell travelling across the kitchen. The thing about chips, he said, is that they must melt the butter on your piece. If they're not hot enough for that you might as well eat them out of the paper. Forget about the bread.

What keeps me going? That I didn't kill the man, that it will all be over some day. I will walk out free. The police won't want me for whatever I was in, whoever was in it won't want me for opting out. And that the girl from the dole loves me. She loves me.

All thoughts stop with Sam.

Short Stories

Homecoming

Soft turned to hard when her foot touched the dappled stone. It was a stone she looked for, knowing it would be there. Stones don't go anywhere. Her foot rested still against the moving water. She was holding her skirt up, holding it bunched in her hand at the front, and testing gingerly whether the other foot would fit on the hard, flat surface.

She listened to the sounds of childhood frolic but they were so deep and muffled, smothered in the brain's blanket. She had to force herself to cry. It would be better. She missed them, missed them all, everybody. But somehow always knew she would be alone.

Her mother had been the only link. She had never recovered from the sudden death, the life that had been hers yet had slipped out without her consent. It was what she had feared from the day she discovered her mother's loneness, the day she understood identity. She had feared it yet denied it could ever happen.

She cried and let her skirt go in the helpless motion, so that the hem became heavy with wet. Lowering herself she let the water cut around her body, so that her bottom clothes were soaking. She remembered carrying home the wet knickers, sneaking them round the back and drooping them on a bush, then casually climbing the stairs to rummage for another pair. The rest had promised they wouldn't tell, not that there would be trouble but it was the embarrassment.

She cried harder at how important it had seemed. And now who cared. Who cared if she lay here and drowned. She might, she had considered it. Considered an end rather than the on and on. It was why she had left them.

Light lowered and streaked beyond the soft Down hills and the settling cattle. There was the dull ringing of laughter in her head, and a misty picture of a stray cow ambling to the bank of the river, plodding down, regarding them suspiciously, but plodding on, disturbing muck and splashing water, then slurping, its big mouth dribbling. Strange beasts, cows, so familiar yet strange.

Dripping from the waist down, she carried her shoes and picked spots between the dung until she reached the stoney bit beside the gate. It was still chained, the rusty chain hanging and clinking when she held the bars. She climbed over and down the other side.

Now, sitting up on the hump of the bridge, she felt descending shadows chilling her shoulders and shivering down through her lower body. She felt them but she had set herself against them, welcoming them, knowing there was no further harm to be done.

Swaying slightly back and forward, her eyes closed, drunk in the continuous sound beneath her, chattering gossiping water. Permanent yet without her now, empty and sickening.

There was no knowledge left, no hope of days that were stretching into a future. No mother for her, no mother for her children. Mothers had died.

A boy's thick thigh sloped down from his bent knee. He was lying back on one arm and sucking a blade of grass. A boy growing up and waiting, with a sophisticated grin. It was summer, real full summer, with long, dry grass and the river low.

She walked towards him, pressing down her dress against her nylon stockings. She looked back once at her cousin who was leaning over the bridge, looking down. She knew then it was no joke. Her cousin, normally a giggler, nodded seriously.

She approached him, the sun blushing her face. She blew upward, her bottom lip out, hoping to prevent the bursting redness which was no longer attractive.

She picked a spot alongside him and settled on her hunkers.

'You came then,' he said, the blade sticking out from the corner of his mouth.

'Yes,' she said, aware of the syllable, the refinement of saying it, the reserve in her lowered eyes.

There was a hum. There was always a hum on hot afternoons, in the grass, a hum and the slow effortless movement of water.

Her cousin had gone.

He was holding her hand when they went towards the gate. And looking down with a new smile.

She swayed in the cold damp, the hard, grey stone now hurting her bones, and yet she was unable to free herself. The dark pain merged with the soft smell of summer grass so that when she opened her eyes she didn't know immediately whether she was feeling good or bad.

She looked drowsily towards the field, the spot, the chained gate, and underlying it was the knowledge of this. As though that knowledge were always there. The only one.

There was a rustle and a cow's long, fading echo, the moo-OO. It was somewhere along the inner side of the wall. Somewhere, wandering, unaware, stupid and lucky. It represented something, she used to think it of cows. They fitted in. There was no conflict with their surroundings.

Now light was scarce, thin on the horizon, and still shapes could be picked out, a hedge, ruined, angled brick on the side of the rising road, the clump of bushes on the summit of the hill, beast bodies mostly at rest. The odd slow, dull plod. It was where she was born, not physically, but it was here she dated her birth, the girl, aware of herself.

Her mother waited in the house above, the big roadside house, full, where she mingled in safety, her short-sleeved, full-skirted summer dress swaying between other skirts around the range. Her cigarette held surely. The whiteness of the sun-yard blaring in. Sticking forks in the huge pot of boiling potatoes. And her grandmother blarging into the middle, snapping the handle of the pot and pulling it off the open top of the fire. They would scatter about as she made her hot, daring dash to the scullery. Limping her limp, but definite as an athlete to the tape.

Her mother laughed softly. It was as if there was no darkness in the city.

They took evening walks round the road as they called it, she and the boy. She felt as if there was nowhere else you would ever want to go, no place, no time. Slow walking and stopping to lean against his white shirt, the wide, low hum expanding, extending out from their warmth. Closing in a kiss.

'I love here,' she told him.

'You're a city girl at heart,' he said, laughing, knowing she hated it, the very sound.

'No I'm not. I'm coming to live here. This is my home, my mother's home.' She was careful not to say too much. Never to say too much.

But Belfast's city lamps were somewhere else, somebody leaned against them making city promises. Somebody waited for closing time, sat in a dreary terraced house, fading lace curtains and worn blinds shutting the yellow light out. Until the key turned in the door.

Her mother buttered bread and talked country talk and saw her come back into the kitchen. She passed through and went up the stairs. Cousins and brothers asked trifling questions. She waved them aside and went over to sit on the white window sill, hugging her knees and looking across the field. She felt their presence behind her, their tension, waiting. 'Oh look,' she said, 'There's a rabbit. Up on the hill.' Then she turned and laughed at all their faces.

It ended because she was too smart for him. Too city smart.

I might take him with me and educate him, she had told somebody.

Her eyes felt puffed and dry now and her body shivered from cold and fear. She eased herself down off the bridge, feeling for her shoes with her feet as she did so. Her legs shook and she stood looking around her, hugging herself and wondering should she make for a hospital or where. Where did you go?

When you had left your children. Watched them wave and smile to your emptiness as they walked out the gate to school.

It had been an emptiness, standing in the kitchen, juggling the dishes in suds and looking at the lined aspect of the houses opposite. A venetian-blinded view. She had never settled to the lack of boundaries but had created her own. Family, past, background, loyalties. But there was always the threat that in this society anything was permissible, desirable. The expected proof of the individual. It had a lot to do with the sixties' confusion and people like the Beatles.

As she stood in her nothing-pale, painted kitchen, idly staring, idly stirring her hands in the detergent-flavoured water she thought vaguely of Eastern society; there seemed comfort in its limits.

The green suds were like the sea, as she rolled them towards herself, glancing down at the home-made frothy waves and then gazing at the still house opposite, the yellow car parked outside its door. Always parked outside its door. Nobody went anywhere.

The phone never rang. Or if it did it was her husband saying 'Well?' To which she usually answered. 'What?' and fixed her hair behind her ears, or ran her fingers round the numbers and waited.

'Just thought I would give you a ring,' he'd say.

She longed for something more.

Names came into her head. People who had lived in patternless dots, down lanes, up hilly drives. Names like the McCanns, people enfolded in their isolation. Whose lights unexpectedly speckled darkness and relieved its oneness. Defied its monopoly, its complete authority.

She looked for the lights now. Straining and rotating she tried to pluck them from the crazy obscurity encircling her.

She thought of the comfort of being taken in. Wrapped beside the range and handed hot tea. Steam and heat fussing about her without criticism or judgement. It was nothing more than childhood's promise.

The taxi swerved and retracked its way, burrowing into the night, its tiny red lights a diminishing glimmer. The hall door flung back and noise and brightness splashed out, greeting them and drawing them. Mother and Grandmother leant and kissed, children waited their turn.

'Father's in the town,' Mother said. 'He'll be out later.'

Up the hall the Christmas tree bounced balloons, shook glossy, coloured balls. She watched her mother step into the kitchen light. It was one of the ways she remembered her.

She stopped and felt the point of nothingness, the completeness of giving herself to its space. Neither going on nor going back. Yet with the enveloping vacantness, her feet were moving, one in front of the other, in a swaying, walking motion. She was making a noise with her mouth, a shivering, despairing moan that would not stop. It seemed to be coming from the road as well, hoarse as the rough, stony surface and renewing itself in the twist of the road.

As she left the house she was unemotional, only a blank dullness behind her eyes and she sighed a lot when she was tidying up bits and pieces, long, scraping sighs, up and down in unmusical rhythm. It had been important to tidy things, to leave no mess behind. She phoned her husband and told him steadily that she had an appointment with the doctor she'd forgotten about. Could he nip out and pick the children up from school. It wasn't unusual. Then she wrote a note for him to find when he returned. It said 'Sorry about this. You were right. I can't cope. Love to my darling children.'

There were no long-term plans. There was nothing except that she was walking out. She took nothing with her except her handbag and a little money.

There was no decision involved in the process that brought her to the top of the hill. It was a hill they dreaded as children.

On a hot summer's day, unshaded and exhausted, they sprawled back on the ditch, panting and throbbing, their bare limbs stretched, longing for home and the gushing pump out the back. Accusing each other of having led the way. Then, trailing with limp limbs, they would take the lane way home, ducking to avoid the glorious, leaning branches which met overhead and protected them from the sun. From the wide, spacious, beating heat.

A line of white, low cottages appeared on the left of the road. She was sitting on the ditch, a little down the hill, looking at their lights and fidgeting for names. The Harveys, was it, and the Donegans.

An old car struggled up, threatening not to make it, with every splutter to stop and maybe roll back down again. She had a vague interest in its progress, anything moving, passing, animated. Then as it approached she regarded it as if it was from her past, her religion. A black and white photo from her mother's album, creating in her a sense of awe, of unchallenged belonging. Unkept promises. She had never said society had let her down, her and her mother before her. Some people could say it and get away with it. But it had never seemed her right. Yet here was proof of it, as was her mother's death, the ultimate proof. She cried after the car, after the failed family structure, her belief. It stopped at the first cottage and a man smoking a pipe got out. He hesitated in the darkness, the tiny glow of the pipe flickering and sucking its renewal and she could make out a dark hat shape at a tilt on his head. She looked straight across at the opposite ditch when she saw him move and heard the hard crunch of country boots coming towards her.

'My goodness girl, what are ye doin' sittin' in the ditch at this hour o' the night?' He leaned down towards her, and she turned to see his puckered concern.

'Eh? Eh?' he waited for some response but she was looking back down the hill, chattering out of her restraint. 'I . . .' she attempted, but there was no explanation for the man beside her, none beyond the helpless, shivering heap he witnessed.

'You're not well, girl, come on in wi' me.' He bent and offered two working hands. She nudged her arm towards them and accepted their support.

A small rectangle of light dizzied her eyes as she struggled to keep her balance through the introduction.

'A found 'er in the ditch. Just sittin' there. The wee girl's not well. Put 'er in the corner there beside the range. Come on, Lizzie, off yer backside.'

A girl, woman, something around her own age, stood before her, uncertain, or unwilling, listening and looking. Children clinging onto her stared up at the strange person, the awkward presence in their small bright kitchen.

'Into the room, all o' yis,' the woman said. They scurried away, joined by Lizzie, a self-conscious teenage girl who left the wooden corner chair.

She seemed to know the children, their dark faces, their brown, sunken eyes. They were drumming in the back of her brain from somewhere far off. They were there before, brown and dark and there was something else about them she could almost remember.

'Tea, Biddy,' the old man said. 'Hot tea for the wee girl. She's not well.'

Biddy lifted a black kettle off the range and disappeared through a low door.

'Don't mind her,' the man said. 'She's got worries. Now tell us yer story.' His eyes probed hers, like beams of sunlight penetrating a deep pool, penetrating the surface, but leaving the depths intact. She stared back, unnerved but unready to open her wounds to the man bent foward, waiting.

Biddy planted the sooty kettle back on the range and beside it a brown and white delft teapot. Her eyes were lowered, suspicious and introverted.

Biddy stood against her. Biddy had worries but Biddy had not fallen, had not failed. Had not, maybe, understood the extent of their devastation. Or was it that she had back-up, that she wasn't alone.

Biddy was part. Part and against isolation. She had never known it, against lonely strangers.

'Are they all yours, those children?' She asked Biddy.

'Them? Aye.' Dusky faces peered round the door, faces smudged, hostile. They offered nothing yet they were not strangers.

Then faintly there was the drone, the long cat-like note of bagpipes, riding the air down the hilly road, piercing blackness. She remembered them, threatening comfort, suggesting the out-there, the loneness of the man who had to play through the night. In bed you worried about safety, vaguely, distantly.

'He still plays,' she said, staring into the fire. But the man was alerted, and Biddy banged a cup on the wooden table.

'Who? Who would you be meanin'? he asked. He was tapping an upside-down pipe on the palm of his hand.

'The man that plays the bagpipes,' she said.

'How would you know anything about him?' the man asked. 'She's not from round here is she, Biddy?'

Biddy handed her a mug of tea. She got her hands round the hotness and watched the steam, felt it on her nose, its dampness rising and entering her pores. She lifted it towards her mouth and drank as though it contained the ingredients of what was lost, the rebirth of feelings deadened by change, by summers and winters that were not the realisation of the dream. But it was only the heat of the tea and the lightness of her brain.

There was Biddy, not swarthy like the children, but dirty fair, comfortably untidy. A little overweight. A woman who had borne several children, who had eased them out as though they were the one child. Biddy who had not considered the trauma of the individual.

No, it wasn't Biddy, not Biddy of the fair look. It was the children, it was the small, dark boy with the matted, black hair, with the eyes that asked a question you wanted to answer.

'Maybe somethin' a bit stronger,' the man said.

Biddy went to a cupboard and lifted out a bottle and a glass. She poured from the bottle, crudely splashing the golden liquid into the glass. She came over and held it towards the intruder who hesitated, looking into her mug, its steam thinly rising, disappearing.

'Gi' me that,' the man said, snatching the mug from her. 'Biddy, get the girl a drop o' water. She won't want that nate, not a delicate lookin' crayter like her.'

'Aye, okay,' Biddy said sarcastically, her voice rising, her irritation just controlled. It was a simmering irritation but there was something attractive. Maybe the limits of her life. Maybe even the bagpipes, the continuity of their hum, the small range of their notes.

She may have walked into the town and out in a twilight. The revolution may have passed her by.

The alcohol swam, joined the main stream of gushing unreality. It was unreal, unreal to be present here, to be unable to speak. She was a freak. She only understood the bagpipes and their memory, the time that she was alive and there were possibilities.

He appeared in the doorway, the swarthy boy made man, the youth with the soft, trembling hand, made hard, made father. The fair woman went towards him and held his arm. 'Thank God,' she said and her whole body sighed. But he was looking at the stranger, the pathetic, humped figure in the corner chair, holding a glass with two hands, and frozen in a demented stare. He was looking at it and trying to narrow a thought.

Children buzzed out around his presence. He patted a couple of heads abstractedly and they disappeared into their low, dim room again. The fair woman looked up at him, unwilling to let go, her expression suggesting it could so easily have been a memory, but it was him. The dark haired bedraggled female untangled her fuzzy memories. 'We had the same brown skin,' she thought.

The old man poked into the redness between the bars at the front of the range, sparking and rattling, leaning forward, his face roasting, toasting, caught in the heat of something beyond his understanding.

'A found 'er in the ditch,' he said, prodding the crumbling redness, prodding the years of tumbling, fading stories. Saying it the way he might have announced the finding of an abandoned lamb, the mystery behind its being. Only there was a comfortable weariness in his voice, in his expressionless eyes. He no longer had to solve the mysteries.

'The city girl,' the young man said from the doorway. 'Well, well.' He poked in his pocket and produced a tin of tobacco.

Then he sat at a square, wooden table and took out paper and started to roll. 'Get us a light there, Biddy,' he said.

Biddy pulled a strip of paper from an old newspaper and held it into the flames. She lit the thin cigarette, then throwing the charred paper on the tiles she stamped it underfoot. She was agitated and stood not knowing what to do.

'In the ditch?' he asked. 'What were you doin' in the ditch?'

'Could I stay the night?' She asked the question out of nothing, no coherent thought, and of no-one in particular. Biddy was closing curtains tight, bolting doors.

'What about up the road?' he asked her. 'The fancy girls swinging on the gate.' It was the same old sarcastic tone, resentment flashing, the resentment that had been lifted in the summer grass, on the dry, prickly ditches.

'It's all closed up,' she said. 'I thought you would have known that.'

'Aye, I did,' he said. 'All closed up alright.' He laughed and flicked ash onto the floor.

Biddy pulled a wooden chair close to him. She rubbed thick, white fingers through her hair, standing an uneven fringe on end, frowning and rubbing her forehead.

'What's this about?' she asked. Her voice was country, from somewhere around. She began to roll from his box. 'Jim, where up the road? Who is she? Is she caught up?'

He sat stubbing his butt in the ashtray. He stubbed it and rubbed it, screwing grey, dead ashes and looking into them, knowing he was being observed by the women, knowing his thoughts were deep, long, dissembling the ashes, parting them, and curiously experiencing a hopeless rebirth.

'Get the tea, Biddy,' he said. Somehow it didn't seem like a command. More an understanding. Something they would come together about later on. 'I'll go in and see them before they go to sleep.'

She shoved her tangled hair back. Her glass was empty and it was time to go. She would have taken the man who was in kissing his brown children. Held his hand. I don't care what you've been, what you are, she would have said on the road. You belong to me, to then. You belong to the moment that doesn't move, doesn't go. Do you know that moment?

'They're after him,' Biddy said to her. 'Maybe you're after him. But I'll have him this night.' Her lips pouted defiantly and she kicked her chair back and went towards a step leading down to a small scullery.

'I'll go on,' she said to the old man. He was examining the red tip of the poker.

'We wouldn't let a dog out at this hour of the night,' he said. Then he held the poker towards her.

'Do you see the red of that poker, girl?' he said, shaking his head as though he were examining a work of art. 'That's the heat of the moment. But,' he added, piercing her preoccupied stare, 'Watch how quickly it cools. Did you see that, did you? Already?'

He threw the poker on the hearth. 'That girl spends her life waiting for him,' he said, indicating the scullery and whispering huskily. 'It's not right, not right, that's what I say.' Then he looked down at her damp skirt, its heavy weight on her legs. 'You should get them wet things off,' he said. 'You'll get your death. Biddy'll lend you things. She can hang them on that wee line above the range.'

They looked up at the line. She looked at the waiting, the day's work. The work she did when she was waiting. Waiting for his darkness, his shadow passing the low window.

One day he waited for her.

'I like those wee lines,' she said. 'My mother had one in the kitchen. A pulley one. Do you know them? She used to lower it and pull hard to get it up with the wet clothes. God, sometimes the muscles were like round balls on both her arms. And then she wound it round and round the hook.'

She smelled the smell of the damp clothes, the clean off-white sheets and the thinning, fading towels. Before her mother got them up sometimes she held them close to her face and sometimes sucked the peculiar wet taste. It was like the woollen gloves she sucked all the fingers out of. It was the ritual, the unaloneness, the religion of child.

She lifted her skirt and sucked the end of it, twisted it tight and winding and sucked the river flow. With her eyes closed she sucked and swayed and hummed a summer tune. There was a vague picture of her own son, standing in his cot, the chewed end of his little blanket wound round his thumb, the flicking noise he made with it against his finger and the other thumb in his mouth. But he was alone, the part that comes after her. Somehow she didn't feel responsible, she wouldn't taint him now.

The man gave her another drink. 'Alright, daughter,' he said, 'We'll ask no questions tonight. In the morning I would say it's the doctor for you. If you ask me, you're wandering.'

'For sure,' she said, drinking and staring at the young man in the doorway again. She flattened her hair back and had fuzzy thoughts of nice people telling her she hadn't changed.

Biddy's sleeves were rolled up. White chubby arms supported a tray of tea things. She was flabby, plain, but it was lovely the way she carried the tray. As if she would never drop it.

'Here, Jim,' she said. 'Come on, Da.'

Jim watched the woman in the corner. He wanted to know why she came here. He wanted to carry her back to the spot, immerse her in the dew. He thought about it, though to watch the way he chewed into the crusts you wouldn't have thought his brain, his mind's colours, could see the sunlight and her shining hair, the venal step of her half-hidden shoe in the grass.

Biddy refilled his cup. She asked him no questions but smiled in a worried way.

The old man looked to the corner and said, as though he wasn't really saying it, 'You wouldn't be wantin' tea.' Biddy ignored him and the woman in the corner shook her head. Jim looked across and several times said 'Ssshh' as if he heard a sound.

'Oh no,' Biddy said and held his arm.

The old man carried on as though it was all irrelevant. One time he turned to the strange woman and said. 'I've lived in this house seventy years.'

'I remember you,' she said, slitting her eyes drowsily.

'Me?' the old man twisted round to her.

'Yes,' she smiled. 'You did the hay. You threw it high with the pitch fork.' She made a half-hearted flinging movement.

But she was smiling wanly towards the young man, his hard thigh moving near the river.

'My mother cycled into the town. It was during holiday times. She wore a light blue flecky coat, do you remember?'

She felt as though she would talk now.

'She used to cycle down the steep hill and I thought, Oh God, I should have checked those brakes. I always thought, God I should have checked the brakes. Did you ever think things like that when people were gone, when you saw them, their physical presence, move away? Did you ever think that? And then know they'd be back and you didn't even have to tell them you were worried. It wasn't necessary after all.'

She rubbed her reddening legs in the heat. 'It's lovely,' she said.

'She's drunk,' Biddy said, sipping from a flowery china cup. 'Drunk or mad.'

'The wee girl's not well,' the old man said.

'It doesn't matter a damm,' Jim said. 'Leave her alone.' His eyes were still the hooded, teasing type, the tempting, dangerous, screwed, gentle type. He was in God knows what.

The girl in the corner cried down her face, cried and contorted for sympathy.

'Could you lend us a brush?' she asked Biddy. 'I had a bag earlier but it's gone. Probably at the river. I only want to look respectable.'

Biddy stared at her but Jim got up and went into a room. He came out with a large hair brush.

'Here, I'll do it,' he said.

Biddy got up and started banging dishes onto the tray. The old man resumed his seat by the fire.

'Did you sleep in a haystack or somethin'?' Jim asked. 'It's all natted together.'

Biddy stomped into the scullery but she never dropped a dish.

His fingers glossed the soft, falling hair, the hair that lay in the green young summer grass, the hair that was washed twice and brushed by the latticed window where the view reached the crossroads.

'It's a bloody mess,' he said.

Many a day it wasn't a mess. It sat still and hopeful by the kitchen window.

'It lost its soul,' she said.

'Where?' he asked.

'Over the green suds, the silent bubbles.'

They were the silent bubbles that renewed themselves every day, yet were nothing, were achieving nothing, except a dish rack of cleanliness.

'Could you call it progress?' she asked the old man. He took his eyes from the red glow.

'I don't know,' she said. 'It's just that a moment progresses but a day doesn't.'

'We're all moving towards the same end,' the old man said. 'It's the building-up of the days you see.'

He was almost interested but Jim tugged hard at the dry locks.

'You're depressing me,' he said.

He never grew up, she thought. The boy who fathered five or six children. Then she knew she had come on purpose, she had been looking for him, for his time, his memory. She knew it would be one of these houses. Things don't change much with his sort. Not roots, homes, families.

The notes of the bagpipes were giving 'Danny Boy' to the night, panting and squeezing it, pressing it up into the stars, the moon, the greatness.

'God, I don't believe it,' she said. 'Not still "Danny Boy".'

The old man laughed. 'Aye,' he said, 'Every night, girl, every night – at the same time.'

'We didn't notice time then,' she said.

'The fancy girls on the gate,' Jim said. He was laughing and jerking at the knots. 'The fair one, the black one, and the brown one.'

She turned to him, smiling out of those evenings. 'Come on,' she said, 'Which of us did you really fancy? really.'

'You,' he said. 'But you let me down. Sending that message up the road and me waiting under the tree.'

She remembered pulling the patterned curtain slightly,

peeping, as her cousin delivered the word. He was smoking, leaning against the ancient trunk, complacent, waiting for her.

'It was your complacency that got me,' she said. 'It was that. You see, you had no right.'

The old man started raking, rattling, shifting in his chair.

'Biddy'll be needin' a hand in there in the scullery,' he said.

Jim looked at the hair, put the brush down and without saying a word went down into the scullery.

'That boy's easy led,' the old man said. He didn't take his eyes off the fire. She too looked into the fading brightness. 'Biddy has enough worries,' he continued. 'The times and that, the situation pulled him in before he knew. It was his friend bein' shot. Wee Tom Duggan.'

'I heard it,' she said. 'I remembered him. He fished over the bridge.'

'The very lad,' he said. 'Over the bridge. A good fisherman he turned out to be. He just seemed to have the knack.'

'I wouldn't hurt a fly,' she said. 'But I've been through a lot.'

She was twirling a strand of hair.

'My husband's good. No, it's not that. And the children. They're lovely, you know.' Tears were there again, rolling down her heated cheeks. But she didn't seem to mind. There was no point in minding now.

'But you see it's what I've lost, what she lost. It goes on and on. It just never stops, in here, you know.' She pointed to her head.

A faintly recognisable air was playing on the bagpipes now, piping, stacatto, lone, endless.

The old man hoked in a cupboard. He pulled out a tartan blanket.

'Could you put some more coal on the fire?' she asked him.

'We usually let it go out,' he said.

'Please,' she said. 'Just for the one night.'

Jim was in the doorway.

'I'll get the bucket,' he said. But the old man was over at his side.

'Don't you go outside that back door,' he said. And he passed him into the scullery.

Biddy came into the kitchen. Her eyes were red but maybe she had just splashed her face under the cold tap.

'I'm goin' to bed,' she said. 'They'll make up the couch for you. We've little enough space, God knows.'

She looked hard at Biddy. 'I'm no threat,' she said. 'Thank you for taking me in.'

'Goodnight,' Biddy said.

The old man rubbed the wooden table with a cloth. It looked like a worn-out vest but it was damp and adapted to its new role. She thought of her mother scrubbing the knarred wood with the hard, bristled brush and the red soap.

Jim built up the fire. The tartan blanket lay humped and untidy in the corner of the patched leather couch. She liked it here. Everything about it. It was what you should be proud of. And the bagpipes, the religious nights, the centring, the warming together.

Jim bent towards her so that she jerked out of her thoughts.

'Don't open the door to anybody,' he said. 'And if you hear anything strange just creep in and warn us.'

'Fine,' she said. Somehow it registered no fear. There wasn't room for it, a new fear, a young fear.

'I'll take you into the town in the mornin',' the old man said. 'The world and its brother's probably out lookin' for you by now.' He shook out the cloth, the old vest, so that crumbs fell on the floor. He went down into the scullery.

'I'll see you in the mornin',' Jim said.

'Okay,' she said. He hesitated. 'It must be fifteen years,' he said.

She didn't answer.

It must have seemed strange to him. Her sitting there in the corner like that when he came in. Like her step through the grass.

Like the bagpipes haunting their hopes. The bagpipes were right and yet the bagpipes had survived.

They had stood looking down the road into the hour of evening, the pink golden hour that changed as you watched and transformed the land. Every minute there were changing shades, fickle and taunting. Taunting the days when teenage girls tease each other with jealousies, but really want reassurance. It's what they had done. Standing on the big gate or sitting on the high wall in tight trousers or light dresses. At the hour when the country boys cycled or drove home from the town. The evening hour. Only she pretended superiority. It seemed required, being the city one, the educated one.

Even then I feared my confusion, she thought. She was under the tartan blanket, dizzy in thought, in memory, and the golden liquor. The room was shadows, shapes and shadows on the ceiling, and the confined, red glow diminished again. Not expansive like the fading evenings, the creeping twilights.

She thought of the woman in her life, the woman who had made her life, and used the tartan blanket to squeeze hard into her eyes until the pressure was sore. She cried with the bagpipes so that they were in low, rhythmic harmony. Controlled in their sorrow, their hopelessness. Because there was something hopeless about the bagpipes. About their very survival. About the man who played them through the night.

They set out in the car. It was a fine morning. She had stood outside the cottage and looked around at the countryside which hadn't changed except for new bungalows rising here and there out of the greenery.

'Where's the lane?' she asked him. But she already saw its overgrown entrance. 'Do children not go down there now?'

'They don't seem to bother.' he said.

She was weak and her body felt as if it didn't fit. But the night and morning had left her with a feeling she couldn't understand, because it was based on optimism. 'I have to go on every day,' she thought, 'like my mother. No matter what it's like. I'm going on. I'm going home.'

Jim insisted on driving her to the town to get a bus. Biddy tried to stop him, but he wouldn't listen. 'I have to go out,' he said. 'I can't hide away the rest of my days.'

Biddy went into the back room and didn't come out to see them leave.

The old man, in wellingtons, jacket and cap, bade her good luck and walked up the road.

They drove down the hill.

'Country cars don't change much,' she said.

He didn't answer and she looked into the side of his face, the proud profile, and she remembered her talk of city life which had provoked his silence.

'I used to tease you and say you're huffing,' she said. 'You always gave in.'

'That's because I wanted you,' he said. He gave her a straight look. 'You know I couldn't believe you went out with me.'

They reached the bottom of the hill.

'Oh listen,' she said, 'Could you bring me back to the bridge? I left my bag there last night.'

He stopped and leaned against the steering wheel.

'I'm serious,' she said.

The car crossed the road and headed straight towards the bridge.

'What brought you here?' he asked. His voice was blunt, almost unfriendly.

'Sadness,' she said.

'You made everybody think you were moving on. You were leaving us behind.'

'It was always like that,' she said. 'It was the cruelty of education and the times. You were shielded here. God, you didn't realise how lucky you were.'

'Why, what happened?' He had stopped just beyond the bridge, at the point where the low wall allowed them to see into the field.

'We all got lost,' she said, 'nothing seemed to work.'

Then she smoothed her hair back and touched his shoulder.

'Have I changed?' she asked him.

She knew she was touching on deeper realms, trying to draw something out of him. But she was sitting in the front seat with him and it was today now, the new day. The freshness of knowing it had moved him seriously those years ago, could keep her going for the rest of her life.

'You look a bit rough,' he said. 'But I'd say it wouldn't take much.'

It surprised her, the closeness, and that she may have said too much. She felt the hotness in her cheeks and wished it was the hotness of that day. She opened the door of the car.

'Mind,' she said back to him as he went to open his door. 'There's a car coming.'

'I'll hold on a minute,' he said.

She strained over the wall.

'I can see it down by the bank,' she shouted back. 'Watch me climbing the gate. Still, maybe you shouldn't.'

She glanced back from the top of the gate. The other car seemed to be slowing down. Maybe fishermen.

She jumped down and ran through the grass, feeling an abandon, and feeling he would be following her.

She lifted the bag which was damp and mucky and turned to see his figure in the field, walking as she had walked that day, moving slowly, hesitatingly.

The sounds she heard and what she saw made her cold and made her grovel in the grass, crawling and screaming. It was the cracking blast of gunfire. It was the countryside split. It was Jim jerking in the air and falling flat. It was the dark shapes of two men above the bridge and then the banging of car doors, and the sound of an engine, screeching into the distant roads, until silence dropped around them. His body still, shattered in the back of the head, blood and flesh and terror.

She lay beside him, praying and asking for forgiveness. Knowing she had been right and that her birth had ended where it had begun. Because all she could do now was weep in the stained grass until someone came to take her away.

X-Days

Saw X today. She was X. It was something I couldn't explain. A mystery and therefore not easy to imitate. It wasn't even beauty. I saw my brother's diary and tried to elicit the secret from him but I was told to mind my own business. I had thought it was my business. It was part of growing up to know why.

Maybe the little curved smile, or the cute way she threw a ball. She was the best thrower in the street. I was a good catcher. I caught it neatly in my cupped hands, occasionally in one, held above my head. I was not to be overlooked, nor as a skipper. Yet somehow nothing got started until her small frame was seen at the top of the street, her long wound rope under her arm, or her three balls juggling in the air.

She was X. In a summer twilight I was sitting on the kerb looking at my legs. I was examining their shape, thinking they looked good around the calves. In ankle socks. Earlier in the day I was dismayed at their shapelessness. I decided it was the mirror.

The street was sad. There was no life, no future. I was crunching dust along the edge of the road. Houses dozed in the sinking light, the warm, weighty sunset. You couldn't see the sun, only a narrow rectangle of pinky glow down between the roofs. You didn't often bother to look up. Sometimes around Beechmount there was a bigger view, a mountain horizon, with a red ball slotting in. Beechmount was out of bounds.

X turned the corner. I couldn't really see what they saw in

her, but I bowed before the fact that it was there. Her aura. I looked up to watch her approach. There were no boys in the street. There was no-one in the street but me. I felt the responsibility of being the only one. Because important people have to be entertained, interested, amused. And X was important. I felt myself blushing. I wished my brother would turn the corner from the entry, his hair quiffed back, his pale mouth shaped in quizzical expectancy. Almost a smile. I wished it not only for my own sake but for his as well. Because he would have a great opportunity now, with no-one else around. In truth I wished X would notice him, pay him more attention. He deserved more than her nonchalant skip, her curious brown slitted glance. He took trouble, combing his hair carefully in the entry, fixing his socks. With a certain loyal disappointment I realised he wasn't first in line. If anyone was. It was hard to tell.

Unsure of whether to greet her in a manner she deserved or to enhance my own self-esteem by ignoring her, I ended up by concentrating more on the dust beneath my feet while recognising her approach with side glances. She carried neither ball nor rope that I could see, but had her hands in the pockets of a neat white jacket. She stood above me.

'No-one around?' she asked.

'No,' I answered with guilt in my voice. Guilt at the lack of others and my own awkward presence.

She was swaying, the flare of her skirt sweeping from side to side.

We did not know each other. Simply members of a group which she, in a way, dominated. She came from somewhere else, where it was not clear, though it was certainly in Belfast. More often than not she stayed with her grandmother and was not ashamed to link her on their frequent outings.

It didn't matter what she did. Because she was X.

I watched shadows falling on red brick. A man came out of a house and walked down the street. He wore a dark cap. I heard a woman's voice shrieking at her children, a muffled shriek from within the walls of their home. It accentuated the strangeness of the evening, the fact that there may be no hope. If I sat there slumped in the dust there would be no hope for me.

I stood up and brushed the back of my dress. There was an insignificant difference in our height, perhaps an inch in my favour. I stood back from her. She examined my appearance momentarily. I examined it in my mind for flaws. After all, I hadn't been prepared for this private audience with her. There could have been dirt on my face, a tear in my dress. I stood exposed.

'Have you got a rope?' she asked me.

'A rope? I have – well – it's not exactly – for two?'

'There's nobody else,' she said.

'I'll run and get it.'

I caught my breath at the corner of the entry, just before I turned. I knew the evening was special and I celebrated it by combing my hair and washing my knees, hurrying and leaving things lying in my wake.

She was still there. With her arm around the lamp post, she was leaning towards the road, staring down.

'Here's the rope,' I said, coming up behind.

'Oh?' She gave a little laugh and took it from me, unravelling it with deft movements.

'I'll call you in,' she said.

I watched the rope swishing past her head, skimming the ground beneath her feet. She gave the impression of not lifting her feet at all and each time she landed softly like a kitten.

'I call in my sister Ann.' My heart had been thumping as I swayed backward and forward waiting for my cue, terrified in case I got caught in the rope. Then we were in unison, up and down together, chanting the rhyme and looking into each other's face. Panting and chanting and smiling at our closeness.

We rested on the kerb. She made snake curves idly with the rope. I watched and was afraid that now it might fail, might never be repeated, that my mother would appear at the entry, her arms folded, calling me in, away from the falling summer evening. And X. Or that I would just sit there with nothing to say and she would be bored.

There was nothing to say, nothing to ask her that wouldn't be trivial. I watched the little gold ring on her finger as she moved the rope back and forward and I noted the sophistication of her closely bitten nails.

'Strange that there's nobody around,' she said, looking up and down the street, drawing the emptiness into her brown eyes.

'It's very funny, isn't it?' I said, feeling the thud of guilt again. I could see it all flittering away and already in my mind I was kicking the yard walls on my way round the entry. I was sitting glumly in the chair in the kitchen and answering my mother in short sentences. I was saying to myself, you're a failure, a stupid failure. Why? and receiving no answer.

We heard a shuffling at the corner.

'There's Billy,' I said. 'He won't get in.'

Billy owned the corner shop. But he drank all day and most of the evening while his wife struggled to keep the business going. Often when she closed the shop she locked him out and he would sit on the kerb, defeated and drunk amongst the children.

'He's an awful man,' X said.

'Yes, he is,' I agreed, although I felt sorry for him, and many an evening my younger brother and I spent with him between us, playing guessing games and tolerating the awful stench of alcohol and the pitiful sight of brown nicotine stains and missing teeth. We were like that, my brother and I. We would put up with anything.

Now, as we watched him turning his key hopelessly in the lock, banging angrily on the window of the shop, smudging Lily's little signs of desperation and faith, 'Bananas 2/6 a pound', 'Ripe tomatoes 2/- a pound', I knew that at all costs I had to protect X from his advances.

He was already blundering towards us, his arms flailing the evening.

'Aw there y'are, Ann. Where's the wee lad?'

'In the house,' I said. I looked at X to see if she was going to turn and disappear but she was regarding him curiously. Then she turned to me.

'He your friend?' she asked me.

'Him? No, he's not.' I said with force. I stood up. 'Come on down the street,' I said to her and she got up and followed me.

'No need te run away. I'm not gonna eat yis,' Billy shouted after us.

The dull hum of dusk met the grey walls of the church, enfolded the church and became its meaning so that entering into the silent darkness there was no surprise, only a tame acceptance of despair. Despair in the very heart of hope, hope that after all this ended we would share in something better. A long thin thought that led to the tabernacle, but only to the tabernacle.

She didn't think that. She looked straight at the altar and arranged her skirt across her knees. She didn't smell of the church but of a field up around the Giant's Foot. It was the same hope but brightly.

'I'm praying for my granny,' she whispered to me.

'So am I,' I whispered back. I wasn't. I was thinking of my mother and her sadness and how we would get out. I was seeing her silhouette against the bedroom window, her response more silent than the lisping of old women, dotted about the pews, fumbling beads through knotted fingers. I was stiffening under my bedclothes, stiffening against his illogical wrath and her unwavering innocence.

I waved back at X as she skipped out of the street.

'Where did you disappear to?' my mother was asking me.

'In the chapel,' I said.

'She's not a friend of yours,' she said, looking down at me with that quiet questioning look.

'She is,' I said.

Mr Maguire was sitting on a stool outside his back door. He was smoking his pipe and had the air of a retired cowboy on the verandah of his ranch. Through the open entry door the clutter of his yard indicated he was a man who pottered. He had two grown-up sons, they probably pottered too, there was nothing else obvious that they did, and a wife who had a drink problem.

'Night,' he said through the corner of his mouth.

'Goodnight, Mr Maguire,' my mother said.

My uncle was burning his sausages over the fire and singing as we passed through into the parlour.

'Down at the chapel if you don't mind,' my mother said to my brothers, who looked up from comics when we entered.

'With X,' I said.

There was no worry because it was not my fathers' night off. My mother sat in her patterned summer dress and let down the hem of my winter coat. Occasionally my uncle shuffled in, singing a French song that went – 'Mama –' then meaningless words running into one another which we often imitated. He would rummage in his cupboard in the parlour where he kept his delft and foodstuffs. Often he left a trail of sugar in his wake as he slithered back to the kitchen to the accompaniment of the cup rattling on the saucer.

We played draughts or a marble game and I played 'The Blue Danube' on the piano before my mother led us up the dark stairs to bed.

'What did she say?' my brother asked me when we were in bed.

'Nothing,' I said.

'She must have said something,' he persisted. He was leaning up over my other brother, looking at me.

'She said she was praying for her granny,' I said.

The two of them laughed and then he said, 'Go on back to your own bed. There's no room here.'

The skim of yellow light across the quilt of the empty double bed and my own single bed beside. The plaster flaking on the high ceiling and oldness speaking eerily out from the walls, from the faded flowers and the damp corners. Her loneliness downstairs. Mine up here. Were we to live and die like this? The dummy grunted loudly on the city road outside, the dummy, capable of nothing and of everything. Epitomising unknown fears. The ones we knew were bad enough.

From the past we made a future.

X's crumpled little red eyes dabbed, stabbed with a white lace handkerchief. She stood beside a glamorous lady who may have been her mother. The priest prayed over the coffin and four men, two stout, hoisted it onto their shoulders. She walked behind and didn't notice that I stood there with my brother. Would we ever get over it? She was being hugged, receiving comfort. There was none for us. 'Granny,' she cried.

In the scullery shadows. Bent in work beneath her refinement I couldn't tell her. It could have been her. It touched me too much. It was always that way. It was delicate beyond words.

The Saturday brasses and the vegetable man with the club foot, with the last of the horses, its head in the bag, chewing away. The vegetables never looked over-fresh but it was a ritual. The few pence were available, poked out of the purse in the noisy Saturday sun.

He shaved sometime around lunchtime, pulling, stretching his chin, singing into the mirror, through the white foam, about the white foam of the sea. Something away off. I sat behind in the chair and tried not to think of Saturday night. Maybe it wouldn't happen.

He set off in jolly form, 'Two minutes,' he said. The distance in her eyes stretched beyond the factory opposite.

Saw X on the Grosvenor Road looking into a shop window. She was wearing white ankle boots.

The babies in the street had brown legs. You would have thought they had just returned from the South of Spain. But it was outside their door or on a lucky day on a blanket in the Falls Park. Their mothers patted their flabby thighs and laughed proudly. Toddlers ran and fell on the dry flagstones, fell with arms outstretched, within inches of flying into and out of the grasp of a father.

Steps were scrubbed for Sunday.

My brother and I pretended we were part. But we had thoughts we didn't share and worries we couldn't voice. He was heavy beside me on the kerb. Sometimes I ran away and stood amongst the others, matching similarities. But I couldn't deny the sight of him, wandering back towards the entry.

X never came around. It should have been good for us, good for me, the competition gone. But that was not the effect. You don't step into someone else's place by the mere fact of their going. You can't fill an empty space because an empty space is empty.

The train sweated into Newry station. It sweated and squealed to a standstill. My brothers and I looked at each other but we didn't say a word. I thought they were pale and somehow small. She moved surely, organising luggage.

The door flung open and the station breezes hurried us, train smells dropped behind us as we fumbled our way onto the platform.

I thought of him in the decadence of a corner pub, of the men spitting and swaying around the doorways. But it wasn't our worry now because she was smiling towards the exit.

The Quibbler

'Like flogging a dead horse,' he said.

'Sure I know. You've said it.'

It didn't mean anything. It probably did to them but not to Malcolm. Nothing meant anything to Malcolm except that Sheila had not turned up and he was running short of money and drink. And his mother would be scurrying around getting the parlour ready, pretending to be uninterested, her glazed eyes staring across at the red brick opposite when they arrived. Not uttering a syllable, begrudging them the space in the doorway to get in. But you'd know by the cushions, their corners up. He never put the corners up. But that's the way they would find it, he and Sheila, and the fire set. Occasionally she would scuffle up the hall and sit opposite them, bolt upright on a straight chair, her hard eyes piercing the window. Never communicating, but talking, to no-one. 'Them lads an' their ball. I'll soon tell thim. Hit this door it did las' night. An' the cheek o' thim, not an ounce o' respect. Git roun' te yer own street, I told thim, but sher ye may's well not waste yer breath.'

He doubted if she would recognise Sheila on the street. Certainly he'd never seen her as much as glance at her. She would sit there until he told her to go back into the kitchen or out to the door again. She needed to be told. The thought irritated him.

Then Sheila's freshness and youth moved in him. Sheila had power. The power to decide not to come, by the look of it, and he'd had four pints, four fat, black pints. Sheila wouldn't like it, not if she arrived now and saw his eyes. They looked perfectly normal to him in the toilet mirror a minute ago but as soon as she looked at him Sheila would say, 'You've had a fair bit' and look away as though it disgusted her. They might spend the rest of the evening quarrelling over the meaning of a fair bit.

'The Quibbler', Sheila called him and said it was his hobby. But in a sense she had stunted it by perfecting the art of walking away. Leaving him, his words pouring like an over-topped pint onto the table. She took it so far, she liked to triumph, control the argument, but it didn't take her long to realise that you can never win with a quibbler. The first day she'd walked away was shattering. It was in the middle of a sentence in the middle of a public house. She threw the chair back in furious frustration and when he saw her swish through the door his mouth was still hanging open. He could remember the very sentence till this day. Had he managed to finish it this is how it would have gone: 'What do you mean I never have any money? It's all relative. In terms of whom have I no money? The third world? [Exit] The down-and-outs in Castle Street? Or are you comparing me with Kevin Murphy?' He still regretted that she hadn't stayed to hear that last bit. In a detached way it could appear to be a reasonable enough retort. But the point was he knew what she meant and what she had said was valid, and instead of answering her in the terms in which she had introduced her point, the argument had raged in vicious circles for nearly half an hour.

Of course this was only one aspect of their relationship.

It was incredible that she bothered with him at all. The day he'd run down Camden Street, his big boots with their metal heel-tips echoing across the terraced street and back, finally catching up with her on the Lisburn Road, do you think he'd imagined she would answer in the affirmative to his request for a date? She said no, she was babysitting. She was craning her neck, not looking at him, watching for her bus. He was persistent. When he had caught sight of her walking down the street he knew nothing could stop him running like an idiot after her. Now at the bus stop she stood casual, unperturbed. Uninterested, with a hint of disdain.

'What about Tuesday night?'

'Oh, here's the bus.'

'Look, can I go up with you?'

'What for?'

He didn't know what for. He did know what for. To be with her.

She glanced into her blue file. Was there something in there? A list? Names? She closed it. The bus had stopped and people were getting off. She stepped on, it was so carefree the way she stepped on. Then, and why still baffled him, she turned and said,

'Maybe Wednesday night.'

That was a long time ago. Almost a year. It was a moment he would remember for the rest of his life. It was still the same, the element of suspense and then at the last minute she would give the word. Another date. But where was she now?

He looked around the bar with an expression of superior inferiority on his face. It was a result of the anomalies in his position. He had stepped outside his background when he had entered university. No, long before that. The lads around the East had howled and clutched at themselves hysterically every time he had mentioned the fact that he intended studying that night. Yet he had gone along to the dances with them and taken girls down the entries too. Usually scrubbers.

His mother had only the vaguest idea of what a university was. She knew it was something important because occasionally when he got home she was in a state of agitated excitement and would point at the television. 'It was on the news,' she would say. 'I seen it. The university.' 'What was it about?' he might ask casually, but this had the effect of sending her into a mood of sullen confusion. 'How would I know?' she would mutter, going into the scullery to get his dinner. 'Some man talkin' about somethin'.' She had, after a time, latched onto the term 'economics', and would often repeat it to the neighbours, who had no more idea than she what it meant, but were all the more impressed by the mystery surrounding it.

A strange woman. They were never close, yet she did everything for him, running round for fresh bread and the paper before he was up. Bringing him his breakfast in bed every morning, and if he had a late lecture he slept on and it sat there and got cold. But you couldn't tell her not to bring it. You couldn't tell her anything. She never listened, just did, did, all the time. Relentlessly following her own pattern. Running here and there, carrying loads, poking in cubby holes for money that his father had hidden. Rather than ask for it.

He lived his life in the parlour, where he kept a collection of records which he played on his makeshift turntable. Here he studied as well, only going into the kitchen for meals, talking to no-one because there was no-one to talk to. When his father came in, usually under the influence, he would crack jokes which only he, himself, understood, and ate the meal set down before him. There were never harsh words, nor ill feeling because each one identified solely with him or herself. Except that Malcolm had grown increasingly aware, and the knowledge annoyed him, that his mother was a slave, and that in her non-communicative way, she idolised him.

He clinked some change in his pocket, then drew it out and examined the coins. Another half pint and that's it. She'd let him down this time. No more of her suburban brightness lifting the dreary street parlour, bringing a fresh atmosphere to the tired Dylan lyrics. Was it last night, Christ that was probably it, he had overdone it for certain.

He brought his half pint down to the table. What was it? There were a few of them in the Students' Union having a drink, and the usual so-called intellectual discussion developed. What it was about was irrelevant but the word he'd got caught up in was 'normal'. Yes, what was normal. Somebody had said something about 'most normal people'. And he'd wanted clarification on the use of the word 'normal'. That was it. 'You know what he means,' Sheila had said quietly to him, trying to nip it in the bud, but no, he was adamant. 'I object to the use of this term "normal people". What is a normal person?' Someone tolerantly gave a definition – 'You know, ordinary, the usual.' 'Ordinary? The usual?' he stormed. 'Who is to judge what is ordinary?' Then Sheila, losing her cool, snapped, 'You certainly aren't. Neither ordinary, nor normal.' 'Are you?' he'd retorted. 'Most people would say I am,' she said, but almost immediately realised she'd fallen in. 'Is what most people say necessarily right?' he turned on her. At this point Sheila rose, lifted her bag; 'What is right?' she said into his face. The others laughed. 'See you downstairs,' she said back. 'That's if you and I agree on the meaning of the word "downstairs".' That was very smart of her, he thought now. He was remorseful when he met her at the door. But the night had been ruined. Sheila said that the discussion had been interesting but as usual he was only looking for an argument. He turned every discussion into an argument for the sake of arguing. He wasn't interested in airing points to find answers, or even in simply delving into topics with other people to establish your own viewpoint above theirs. No, it was a case of pick on a word, any word, and refuse to let people get past it. It was hopeless.

He agreed. He would really try the next time. She was to tell him when to stop. He would obey her. He would do anything for her.

The pub was filling up. It would soon be bunged, bodies everywhere, standing all around the bar and someone would ask for the chair beside him – 'Is anyone using this chair?' 'It depends on what you mean by using. I mean you can see that no-one is actually sitting on it.' No, still, he wouldn't. He wouldn't say that at all. He would simply say 'No', and the chair would be removed. He probably would not be here that long, in any case. He fidgeted with his half empty glass. Or was it half full? Whatever it was now, he would leave when it was empty. He could wander up to the Union, sure to be somebody around, or maybe just head for home, across the wet streets to the East. His mother would be standing at the door. She wouldn't ask any questions but she would look at the space beside him and know he was alone. He had done it this time, no doubt about that. How could a girl like Sheila put up with him? Why would she waste her time? She was probably laughing with her brothers up there in suburbia. Joking in the sitting room of her semidetached house, in the armchair with her cup of tea, and the rhododendron bush gently blowing and glistening in the rain outside the window. She might be listening to one of her Beethoven LPs, her shoes off, feet tucked up, and wait a minute, who was that in the chair opposite her?

He sank the last mouthful, flung back his chair – 'Have them both' he snarled to an innocent bystander, and stormed out.

He hadn't even the bus fare left but who needed a bus when the motive was so strong? It was only four miles and the rain was soft, almost pleasant. Hands in his jacket pockets, with youth and determination backing him, he stamped the miles behind. Impervious to the elements, the passers-by, anything except his imagination, he crossed street after street and about halfway he was startled by a shout in his ear. 'Hey, Maguire, what are you up to?' He didn't turn, but the owner of the voice was now walking beside him.

'You're in a bit of a hurry.'

'I am.'

'Hang on. Are ye goin' te yer girl up the road?'

'I might.'

Macdonald had probably nothing better to do, never had, and seemed intent on accompanying him. His big splayed feet sprinkled wet to either side.

'How's the studyin' goin'?' he said and laughed up into the drizzle.

'It's going fine, just fine,' Malcolm said, intensely irritated and quickening his step in the hope of shaking off the idiotic Macdonald. But Macdonald had long legs.

'Y'a a doctor yet?' he persisted.

'I am not going to be a doctor,' Malcolm said. Then he stopped and looked up at Macdonald's hanging jaw. 'Look, do you mind,' he said, 'I'm in a hurry. We can discuss my career at a later date. I'll call down some night. Okay?'

Macdonald looked downcast, but then Macdonald always looked downcast. He turned his collar up. 'It's rainin',' he said, holding out his hand as though to catch some and prove it.

'Your acumen in matters meteorological leaves me stunned,' Malcolm said, sighing sarcastically. 'Goodnight.'

He didn't look back but he sensed that Macdonald stood uncertain for some time before making his way down the road again.

Malcolm felt his nostrils reacting in an unhealthy manner as he steamed past the cemetery. The dead, unaware of the urgency of his mission, slept on. No skeleton rattled on the other side of the wall but a drunk across the road sang mournful songs as he battled with the laws of gravity and completed the double trick of drinking from a bottle while he sang. He lifted his leg high in an effort to cross the road when he spotted Malcolm. Probably with the intention of imparting some vital information, for he had his hand in the air, waving in a gesture of importance. But Malcolm hurried on, in no mood to be delayed. He pulled a crumpled hankerchief from his trouser pocket and wiped the whole of his face.

At the bottom of her street he slowed his pace and thought, 'What am I doing?' The light was on in the front room and he had a crazy fear that her father would open the door and flatten him. Jesus, it must be around midnight now but the increasing sobriety he had felt during his walk in the rain was now being overtaken by an intoxication of frustration, annoyance, nervousness and other feelings too complex to disentangle in his blurred brain.

He had his head down as he stood waiting at the door. A pathetic, soaked figure, breathing heavily through widening and narrowing nostrils.

It was her.

'My God, Malcolm, what's wrong? What are you doing here?'

'Both – questions – warranting – the same – reply.' He needed a breath between each word.

'What is wrong – is that you did not turn up – to meet me. That is – also what I am doing here.'

'Meet you?' She had on little turquoise slippers. He had never seen those before but then he rarely got his foot past the doorstep, did he? 'Why should I be treated like that?' he thought. 'Have I not earned my place in the world? Anybody's world? Am I not a university student?'

'Can I come in? I am rather wet.' He shook his jacket and drips fell onto the step.

'Come in,' she said. He passed her, into the warmly-lit hall. The kitchen door was open and he could see one of her brothers fidgeting at the fridge. He had a flash of his mother sticking meat and things into that old cupboard under the sink. 'Keeps thim fresh,' she would say with pride.

'Hi,' the brother said out.

'Hi,' Malcolm scowled.

She opened the sitting room door. 'Nobody in here,' she said. She closed the door after them. 'Give me that jacket and I'll put it at the fire.'

He removed his jacket and handed it to her. She placed it over a fire guard. Then she looked at him and said, 'You've had a fair bit.'

He sat in an armchair. 'The bit that I've had was not fair at all,' he said. He was smoothing back his wet hair. 'The reason it was not fair is that you were not there.'

She sat on the arm of another armchair. Only on the arm, he thought, because she wants me to go. She looked so lovely, nothing would ever go wrong for her. Nothing would.

'Do you want to know why I was not there?' she said and an amused smile gently shaped her lips. Just gently. Her turquoise feet were crossed. He wanted to eat the slippers.

'I do,' he said.

'I was not there because I was not supposed to be there. Not until tomorrow night.'

He was suspicious. She was laughing.

'Wednesday night we said,' he said firmly.

'This is Tuesday.' She was laughing blatantly now and in danger of losing control.

'It can't be,' he said weakly. 'Yesterday was Tuesday.'

'Monday.' She sank into the chair.

'Sshh,' he said leaning over. 'You'll have them in. Look –' he attempted to clear his brain but now it could be Saturday for all he knew.

'Brian,' she called.

'What are you doing?' Malcolm straightened himself in the chair. 'Look, what are you doing?'

Brian, a tall schoolboy, stood looking in at them.

'What?' he said.

'Brian, what day is this?'

Brian looked bemused but answered unhesitatingly. 'Tuesday.'

'Thank you, Brian,' she said. Brian shut the door.

Malcolm was overcome with embarrassment. The insult of it. He got up.

'I'm going,' he said.

Sheila rose and came over. Protectively she said, 'Sit down and get dried and I'll get a cup of tea.' It was a tone he couldn't resist. It might have been 'Come to bed'. If only it was. When she was out of the room he looked into the fire and then took out his comb and combed his hair. He spat into the fire and said 'Silly wee bastard' at the thought of Brian standing there in the doorway in his supercilious pose. 'Tuesday.' Tuesday indeed. If he'd even thought of saying something to him like, 'Who taught you the days of the week? Was that this week's lesson in school?' What's the point, he would probably have had a smart answer ready.

The toast had heavy, melted, yellow cheese on it. It drooped in your hand when you lifted it. He didn't feel like eating but it was part of something she was offering him. He hoped it wasn't sympathy pure and simple, and his position at the moment was confused; sitting here on a night that had not been allocated to him, he was an intruder. There was an uneasiness in her manner. She left the room frequently – some unfinished business with the family, he supposed. Yet she was effusive in a way towards him. 'Enough toast? More tea? And you sat there all night on your own. I can't believe it.'

'Jesus, it's incredible,' he kept repeating, shaking his head.

'And you walked all the way.'

'All the way.'

And all the way back. He was in no mood to scrounge for the taxi fare and the last thing he wanted was to go at all. The whole thing was ludicrous, farcical. There'd have to be a better arrangement than this.

He moved over onto the couch.

'Come over here,' he said.

She got up but instead of going over to him she lifted the cup he had left on the hearth.

'You haven't finished your tea,' she said.

'Damn the tea. Come over here.'

Uneasily she sat on the edge of the couch beside him.

'You can be very gruff,' she said, not looking at him, but staring at her knees.

'Gruff, now how was I gruff?' he demanded.

'Your tone of voice.'

'My tone of voice? What about the night I've just spent? Waiting for you.'

'That was your mistake.'

'Oh, my mistake. My mistake. So you were not involved?'

'Stop it.' Sheila stood up. 'I'll see if I can scrape together your fare home.'

He relented and, getting up, held her back before she had reached the door.

'No, look, I'm sorry, sit down, just for a minute. I'm going in a minute.'

She sighed and sat down.

'What's wrong with you?' he asked her. He was trying to look into her eyes. But it was difficult. She was pouting and determined to watch the dying embers and she was in bad form. He'd put her in bad form, cast a shadow over the carefree night she'd been having at home – her natural environment.

'Why don't you tell me to piss off,' he said, glumly joining her in watching the flickering ashes. 'Why don't you, for once and for all?'

'Sshh, keep your voice down,' she said. Then she turned and her expression had lightened, for this was a mood with which she could deal. She kissed his mouth. 'I'll see you for lunch in the snack bar tomorrow. And tomorrow night we'll go out.' She was sorting it out. She was irresistible. She would never tell him to piss off. She would have him hovering but, when at his most fragile, would welcome him back.

'I need you,' he said, holding her close to his chest.

She rested there for a moment, then looked at him, tipped his nose and shook her head. But she was smiling, treating him like a schoolboy who had erred but who was eminently lovable. When she left the room, just as she was closing the door she gave him a delightful wink and he sat there feeling like a favourite teddy bear until she returned.

She was holding a fistful of change.

'Here,' she said, 'I scraped around. Didn't want to make it obvious.'

He took it and put it in his pocket. He would have to get a grip on his situation. Stretch out his grant so that it lasted more than two weeks. But Sheila was a student too. She understood. Sheila understood him.

'Madam, it would give me boundless pleasure if tomorrow night culminated in a visit to our house,' he said to her at the door.

'Go home,' she laughed and teasingly pushed him off the step. He waved and trundled off down the street. Brian came to the door in time to see him disappear around the corner.

'What a walk,' he said. 'Is he going to lurch the whole way home?'

'Mind your own business,' Sheila said and shut the door.

As the taxi drove down the road he saw the dripping Macdonald standing at a corner engrossed in conversation, if one could describe it as such, with two old men. What a bloody lout, Malcolm thought. He was worlds away from Macdonald, from them all, and as soon as he got his degree he would be leaving the city forever. It was bearable only because it was no longer a chain. He was tasting the wider world, at university, and with Sheila, on the outward route, and these dank streets were prickles of his past. A few couples waited gloomily for taxis in Shaftesbury Square. He regarded the straggly queue. They weren't like him and Sheila. They were going and coming on a small, depressed scale. They were riveted to their roots. You'd know to look at them.

'This'll do,' Malcolm said just over the bridge.

'Right son.' You were always 'son' in Belfast and girls were 'daughters'. They wouldn't even grant you your right to have grown up.

A girl in very high heels and a tight coat approached him. Her hair, swept up into a bun, was fair and wet. She glanced at him as he passed. Something made him turn and look after her and when he did so he found that she was looking back at him. She stopped. 'Got a light?' she said, tentatively.

'Yes,' he said, 'I have.' He took his lighter from his pocket and she came back and bent over to receive the flame. He shielded it from the rain with his hand, at the same time examining her face. She was very young and her hand shook. He couldn't help being struck by her features, pretty and perfect, and by her nearness to him.

'It's late to be walking on your own,' he said to her.

'Had to get out. Them.' She directed a glance towards the Newtownards Road. 'I can't stand it.'

Anything she said might or might not be true. In fact it almost certainly would not be true, but the face and body before him were not fictitious. She made no move to go. Malcolm's brain churned out several thoughts, like that his parents would be well in their beds, and that his metabolism had been aroused to expect something this night. Not that that something would be the same thing, but there was a young girl before him. In any case the least he could do was offer her a bit of heat and a cup of tea. It would be a good deed – if nothing else.

'Look,' he said, 'I live round here. Would you like to come in out of the rain for a while?'

She stared at him out of wide eyes, but made no response.

'Come on,' he said.

She tripped along beside him and as they entered the street the fluttering inside him was fighting with itself. He fumbled for his key and she pressed in beside him. It could have been boldness or a desire for protection. He didn't know.

'Do you live on your own?' She asked him. In the lamplight her face was pale and winsome.

'No. They'll be in bed.' If they heard voices they would assume it was Sheila with him. They knew not to interfere. He came and went as he pleased. His mother might shout down occasionally, 'That you, Malcolm?' 'Yes,' he would respond and she would shuffle back into bed. Maybe she never slept until he came in, maybe worried constantly about his well being. But what could he do about that?

He drew the blinds and put on the light. The fire was set but it was too late for that now. He plugged in the electric one, and took off his jacket, self-conscious now in the brightness. He'd been meaning to buy a lamp for the parlour, he'd talked it over with Sheila but they hadn't got around to it. The crude light hung from the centre of the ceiling, defying any subtle approach to the young girl he had brought home.

She was sitting on the couch, damp tights clinging to her legs, her eyes perusing the room. He was afraid suddenly that she was a child, a baby who had run away from home, that he should take her to the police station. Yet she had obviously spent some time preparing – red shaped lips, black mascara, some of which had smudged in the rain, or had she been crying?

'Look, what age are you?' he asked her, trying to sound casual. He was bending over, choosing a record.

'You've a cheek,' she answered. 'But I'm nearly nineteen.'

She could be, she couldn't, but bar asking her to produce her birth certificate. . . He chose Bob Dylan. As soon as the words poured out he regretted it – 'Shut the light, shut the shade, you don't have to be afraid' – and yet it helped him, a mood rippled, encouraged him. There was no contradiction, no shame. Sheila sitting there and this girl. He turned to her, kneeling on the floor in front of her – 'Kick your shoes off. . .' the song went.

Colour was rising in her cheeks with the heat from the bars and then she had her shoes off, she was peeling down her tights, unveiling slowly her statuesque legs. He knelt back and watched. What else could he do. She threw her coat to the other side of the room. Her dress was skimpy. Before him she rose and, going over, turned off the light so that the room was only lit with the red glow from the electric fire.

'You're a student,' she said. She was leaning against him from behind, fingering his hair.

'How did you know?' He found it difficult to talk with the constriction in his throat.

'Books,' she answered. She was massaging his neck now.

'And you?'

'Me?' she said. 'I'm just a little girl who has problems at home.'

On the floor she clung to him. She cried into his body and he caressed her and told her it was alright. There was nothing to cry for. He rejoiced in kissing the tears and Bob Dylan sang on. . . She was no baby. She was a little fox and he was the innocent one, the chicken. But it didn't matter for in the end they were sighing together.

He was lying on the couch. She had turned the record over and was sitting beside him, dressing.

'I'd better go,' she said. 'It'll be alright now. He'll be out cold by now and she'll have stopped her whingin'. They'll leave me alone till the next time. Thank you.'

'Thank you? No, look, lie down for a while. Have a rest. You can't go up there on your own at this time. And in the rain and all. As soon as it's dawn I'll walk you up. Look, stay.'

She stopped what she was doing and stroked his forehead. Her hair was all down around her shoulders and Malcolm thought she looked like a dreamy angel.

She lay down beside him.

'Alright,' she whispered. 'We'll sleep for a while. Just a wee while.'

There were things to be worked out in the morning but for the moment it was nice, so bloody comfortable.

Malcolm woke and raised his head. It was the parlour he was in and there was a peculiar smell, an unfamiliar mixture of perfume and. . . good God where was she? He was alone. What time was it? My watch, where did I leave my watch? Christ. He frantically fumbled around the couch, crawled across the floor. The watch Sheila bought me for Christmas – no, the bitch, she didn't, she wouldn't. The bitch, after me taking her in out of the rain.

The only relief walking through the town and up towards the university was the cool breath from the autumn breeze. It blew away something. There was the watch, two of his favourite LPs, including the one he'd played for her last night, his mother's old clock, about the only valuable thing she owned, how under God was he going to explain that. There was no way, he'd pretend he knew nothing about it, and possibly a couple of brass candlesticks. He couldn't swear about those.

He blushed at his stupidity and the thought of his sleeping simple face as she made off with the loot.

And Sheila, oh, Sheila. It was your fault. No, it was my fault. No, it was the day's fault. It should have been Wednesday. Why was it not Wednesday?

The snack bar was normal. Chaotic, loud, gushing, intellectual, colourful, pseudo-everything, and normal.

'Sheila, I'm sorry. Sheila, will I get you something? Look, come on up with me Sheila.'

The others looked at him. He didn't care who looked at him. He needed only Sheila to wash away his sins. They would go into the Botanic Gardens after and sit amongst the flowers. That's what they would do.

Sheila got up and gave her friends a knowing look. Up at the counter she said, 'What's wrong, Malcolm? You're in a state. Did you get home alright last night? What's wrong with you?'

'Nothing, look nothing. Look, forget your two o'clock lecture, will you? We'll go out. We'll celebrate.'

'I don't mind about the lecture. I hardly ever go anyway. But celebrate what?' She put a scone onto a plate and lifted another one for him.

'Tea?'

'Yes.'

'Celebrate what?' she repeated.

'I don't know. Anything. Today, tomorrow. Anything.'

'Okay,' she said. 'I don't mind.'

Sheila sat on the grass and sucked a blade. She had her shoes off and she was relaxed. She had a healthy attitude towards lectures, towards the whole damn thing. He kissed her on the cheek several times. She didn't change her position. She was demure, not the demonstrative type in public, nor in private come to think of it. But she had her way. Sheila had her way.

'Look, Sheila, I scrounged a few bob, we'll go down to the Club after a while and have a drink.' He needed a drink, but only if Sheila came too.

'Maybe so,' she said.

Sheila don't commit yourself. Never commit yourself whatever you do.

'Sheila, do you know what it is to love somebody?'

Sheila turned sharply, reacting quickly to the inferred accusation.

'Love somebody? Of course I do.'

'Then who do you love, Sheila. Tell me who you love.'

'It depends on what you mean by love,' Sheila said.

'You know what I mean by love. Everybody knows what it means.'

'But each person may have a separate definition. Your idea of love may be different to mine.'

'Sheila, do you know what you are doing? You're quibbling.'

'Am I? Well isn't that a change.'

'I love you.' He was looking seriously into her face. Didn't he need reassurance, affection, after what he'd been through?

Sheila was fixing on her shoes. 'Come on, we'll have that drink,' she said. She got up and they walked together down the road.

'Let's have a discussion,' Peter Robinson said as soon as Malcolm and Sheila walked into the lounge.

'Yes,' Barry McCullough said. 'Upon what academic topic should we ponder? What do you think, Maguire?'

'Give us a break,' Malcolm said, selecting a table some way away. 'What do you want Sheila?'

'A beer,' Sheila said. She was smiling over at them. In a way she would have liked to have joined them.

'I know,' Robinson persisted. 'A word. We'll select a word. Discuss it, dissect it. What about it, Maguire?'

'Whatever you like,' Malcolm said back from the bar. 'Just so long as you don't expect me to buy you a pint.'

'Do you see the name you've got for yourself?' Sheila said when he sat down beside her.

'Name,' he said, lifting and sipping. 'What's in a name?'

'There can be a lot,' Sheila said. She was doing it again, looking past him. If he told her it could have the effect of shocking her into committing herself. He would know where he stood then. She was too sure of him, maybe that was it. So confident she didn't even find it necessary to look into his eyes. Well, he would tell her about it.

'Sheila?'

'Yes?' She looked at him, then away.

'Sheila. . . what colour are my eyes?'

'What?' she laughed. 'You're mad. What a question.'

'What colour are my eyes?'

'A sort of greeny-blue. More green in the sunlight.' She still did not look at him but she was right.

'Do you like them?'

'What?'

'My eyes. Do you like them?'

'Malcolm –' She was on the point of laughing, being flippant, but the earnestness of his expression stopped her, in a way startled her.

'I like them,' she said, leaning over and giving him her full concentration. 'Yes, they're serious, and quite deep, really.'

'Deep,' he repeated. 'Do you mean deep or deep?'

'I do,' Sheila said. There was an enveloping quality about her reserved relaxation.

'Did you notice that our sense of humour is compatible?' Malcolm asked her.

'I noticed that mine is,' she said. Then she got up. 'Mind that file, I'll be back in a minute' she indicated her blue file with its various notes which rested on the table.

When she was gone Malcolm sat back and considered the fact that with Sheila there was an ambiguous clarity. You felt good, optimistic with her although her own intentions were obscure. And what was last night? There was only one thing to be said about last night. It was gone. The past.

When he walked home the autumn mist settled around his shoulders and he felt set in his time, a part of today. Comfortably moving along. When he entered the streets of the East he heard distant melodies of his childhood, saw himself in boys running past. It was all necessary really, he thought, and then, realising that thought was superfluous, he smiled and kicked a can along before him.

She was scuttling around the house, muttering angrily into the dotted breast of her apron.

'I seen thim, think I didn't, bifore ma very eyes. The dirty blackguards, snakin' away with it up 'is coat, that big skinny rake was. . .'

He had an impulse to run back down the street. If he'd thought he should have foregone his dinner, grabbed a bite in Dirty Joe's. Saved himself the agony of this. The nuisance of listening. He knew he didn't have to say anything. She never expected him to say anything, but he would hear her problems, the trials of her day. And occasionally, despite himself, he offered half-hearted advice.

On this occasion it appeared to him that it would be advantageous to show some slight interest.

'What are you talking about, Mother?' he asked her as he rinsed his hands under the cold water.

'A'm talkin' about that clock,' she said with renewed vigour. 'That's what a'm talkin' about. That parlour clock yer Uncle John left me. An' them hoodlums that came up that hall an' stole it bifore ma very eyes.'

'You saw them?' he asked. He was settling down to the dinner she had set out.

'Didn' a see thim runnin' down the street?' she said, standing back, her hand on her hip and regarding him incredulously.

'You saw the clock?' he asked, confident of his own position and merely testing her out.

'What?' she said by way of delaying her reply. 'Didn' a see 'im with it up 'is coat?'

'How do you know it was the clock?' He felt there was a slight suggestion of meanness in his stance, but there was no other way, and she was getting a certain amount of satisfaction from the validity of her annoyance.

'An' what else would it be? Is the clock in the parlour? Go on, you see if it's still in the parlour.'

'If you say it's not in the parlour, then it's not in the parlour,' he said. He just wanted to be left alone now to enjoy the remainder of his dinner.

'Well, then,' she said smugly. 'That's proof enough, isn't it, an' if you were half a man you'd go down to the polis for me an' report it.'

This jolted him and caused him to pause.

'Look, we'll leave it for tonight, maybe it'll turn up,' he said.
'Turn up,' she muttered in exasperation as she went off to her lookout post in the hall. ''E doesn't believe a word a'm just after tellin' 'im.'

The clock faded. The whole incident faded. His mother got the most out of it. Played it and replayed it until the record scratched. Standing at the door, hurling abuse at the handball players, seeing the guilt in their faces, amazed at their boldness, continually demanding the return of the clock – 'Now yous'ns have that clock back here by the 'morra night or yis'll be sorry.' They were never sorry, and became convinced that she was mad. The neighbours, having been told the whole story, individually and in groups, clubbed together and bought her a new clock. The fact that they would do this, that they thought so much of her to do it, made up for the sentimental value of the clock she had lost, and it was with considerable pride that she pointed to her latest acquisition now occupying the centre of the parlour mantelpiece.

Malcolm nursed more serious worries now. Sheila had seemed to draw him to her. In his parlour in the firelight she did not only allow him to hold her close. She held him close. She stood vulnerable by the window and playfully released her independence, and at night when he left her home she was loathe to leave him; she stood on, talking, allowing him to hold her hand, even kissing him on the street. And looking back when she left him. He had been led to muse on his good fortune as he tramped the few miles home or sat in the taxi. She wasn't putting it into words but anybody could see that she was giving in, accepting that love is stronger than superficial ideas concerning identity and situation. She wasn't putting it into words but her messages were brilliant. Who needed words?

But words, when they came, shattered his illusion. They were having a drink and she was uneasy. Not unfriendly, but guilty somehow.

One sentence separated them.

'I am going to England,' she said. She couldn't be. Not going to England. Maybe going, but not *going*.

'Going?' he asked, trying to hide his weakness.

'Yes,' she said. She was quiet, not triumphant. Simply stating and concerned. Yes, concerned.

'What do you mean, going?'

'To work.'

'To work? But you're only in your first year. How can you? Look, be sensible.'

'No, Malcolm, there is nothing you can say. I have to go. I can't stand this place, this university. I want to go away and work.' There was a combination of nervousness and release in her voice.

Malcolm was sure of his position. He would do his best to talk her out of it. He had to. It was his duty as well as his desire.

'You are being flighty,' he said.

'Well then, I want to be flighty,' she answered. He put forward the line about throwing away her opportunity of a degree, and what if England didn't work, she wouldn't get back into university. But as he spoke the realisation dawned on him that you can only influence someone who has not yet made their decision.

'What about me?' he asked her. He was looking into his beer. Sympathy at least he deserved.

'It doesn't affect my feelings for you,' Sheila said.

'Probably not. Because it couldn't. You had none in the first place.'

After this their meetings were a combination of tenderness and coolness, unworkable plans and silences.

He left her to the airport all the same. While they waited they had a couple of drinks and he watched her, glimpsing her confusion. Was it adventure? Escape? Sensible? Silly? But she was brave, he would grant her that. And he admired her. And loved her.

He kissed her at the barrier but she was strained. Then, just as she turned to go she whispered to him, 'You know I do love you, Malcolm. See you.'

He panicked. A combination of the couple of pints, the atmosphere, the words he had waited to hear for so long, whatever, resulted in him racing to a window. He saw her coming out onto the tarmac and walking across towards the plane, and with sweat on his forehead and inside his clothes, he began banging on the window. 'That's not love,' he shouted. 'You can't call that love, Sheila. What is it? You tell me.'

Amazed travellers stared at him as he rubbed his breath from the window.

Sheila turned on the steps and waved down, although she saw no-one.

'Do you know what I did one night, Sheila?' he shouted. 'Do you know?'

He waited until the plane door closed and then, turning, he surged through his baffled audience, and saw only the glass door ahead.

Cora's Plight

Hanging under the fresh, flouncy set, Cora's expression seemed to beg forgiveness, plead for happiness and finally settle for hopelessness. In an irritable gesture she flung the baby-pink brush onto the dressing table, upsetting bottles, and crumpling the white lace mat.

'Perfect,' Josephine said. She retrieved the brush and gave a few light, creamy touches to the whisked waves.

'What's perfect?' Cora muttered, planting her chin on her hand.

'Your hair. It's just right,' Josephine said. She gave a little skip across the room to demonstrate her confidence in the situation. Although in all honesty she thought the whole thing was pathetic. Anyone who had to write to those places to get a man must be in a bad way which of course Cora was. And the man, having taken the same course, couldn't be any better. Two hopeless cases trying to make a go of it together. What a recipe for success. The only slightly redeeming factor was that once you reached Cora's age – she must be all of thirty-five – anything must be better than the prospect of spending the rest of your days alone. Josephine's situation was so different. Young, attractive, educated, independent. Imagine having none of these attributes. In fact Josephine's willingness to help and good humour in doing so were in no way related to her faith in the outcome of the venture. Rather they could be said to have arisen from her delight in comparing her own position with that of the unfortunate Cora. Of course she would set her hair, advise in the application of her make-up, trying not to overdo it. But Cora was one of those females on whom make-up had to be spread generously in all its colours and textures. Or else there was no point in using it at all. Cora had no natural beauty. Without her foundation cream, her powdery powder, her bright blue eyeshadow, her shocking pink lipstick, she was like a blank page. With it she was a woman who was interested enough to colour it in. It may never be a work of art, but the effort was there for all to see.

Josephine bent down so their heads were together. She smiled into the mirror.

'Now,' she said. 'You look great, don't you?' At the same time she was wondering how Cora could bear not to be the owner of the face which smiled so attractively beside her own. She must hate me, Josephine thought.

But Josephine with all her intelligence, her education, misunderstood Cora. For Cora was not jealous of Josephine's beauty. She scarcely saw it. Her introversion was such that when she looked into that mirror all she saw was herself, her past, her failures, her depressions, her suicide attempts. She was obsessed with her suicide attempts and was adamant that she would try it again. She was able to quote statistics to corroborate her statements. Josephine was convinced that she would try it again and in fact her enthusiasm for getting Cora matched up was also a result of her terror of being the one to find her in the bathroom with slashed wrists or lying with the empty pill bottle beside her or, worse, spattered on the pavement outside the house.

Cora put her white, nail-bitten hand up to her mouth and began to whimper, at the same time continuing to look herself in the eyes.

'I can't go down,' she simpered. 'I can't. It's no use. I can't start up with another man. I'm going to kill myself, this time I am.'

Josephine adopted a businesslike tone. 'Now Cora, get a hold of yourself. You're working yourself into a state. It's only a matter of control. Once you've got the initial meeting over everything will be easy. Wait till you see. And look, think of it this way. If you don't like him you're under no obligation ever to see him again.'

Cora stood up in her little mules. Her dress sense is terrible, Josephine thought. I know she's no teenager but she doesn't have to dress like an old maid. Cora faced her. She gesticulated with her perspiring, shaking hands.

'Well what,' she said breathing quickly. 'What if I do like him and he never wants to see me again? What if that happens?' Her voice was rising towards a shriek.

'Sshh,' Josephine whispered, 'For God's sake he'll hear you.'

Cora continued in a slightly lower voice. 'Because how could he like me?'

How could he, Josephine thought.

'How could he? I won't even speak to him. I won't. I'll never trust another man after that bastard. . .'

'Now,' Josephine said firmly. 'Stop. There's absolutely no point in going over that again. It's finished and until you put it out of your mind you'll never be able to approach anything positively.'

Josephine was quite pleased with her handling of a very delicate situation. Not being qualified in psychiatry or any related subject. It was wonderful what you could do when faced with a crisis. With common sense and maturity. It was just a pity there was no-one around to observe. It would be left to herself to recount the tale to others, and boasting was not altogether desirable. Although there could be ways of slipping it subtly into the overall story of Cora's misfortune.

Cora flopped back onto her chair. She was sobbing now. Her nose was red and wet and she was trying, unsuccessfully, to dab her eyes without disturbing the eyeshadow and mascara. She resembled a mucky puddle in a watery sun.

'The way that bastard let me down,' she sniffed. 'After all I did for him. And he took all my Frank Sinatra records with him. Every one.' She was shaking her head convulsively. Josephine knelt down and looked up at her. 'I tell you what,' she said, 'We'll go into town tomorrow. We'll buy a Frank Sinatra LP. Your favourite one.'

Cora nearly exploded. She spluttered and spat so that Josephine jumped back quickly and stood up. 'I don't give a damn about Frank Sinatra. It's him, it's him. Do you think I could ever listen to Frank Sinatra again?'

'No, no of course not,' Josephine said. She walked over to the window and looked out onto the street. His black Morris Minor sat pointing down. Towards where? She had left him in the living room, confidently watching television. Smiling broadly. Thinking now, she supposed, it was the usual story, the woman keeps the man waiting. Due to her elaborate preparations. But there was a point beyond which she, Josephine, could not go. After all she was an outsider in effect. It was unfair. She'd already given up a week of social engagements to sit in with Cora, talk to her or rather listen to her. She knew her life story intimately. Cora could trace back the reasons for everything that had happened to her. The focal point appeared to be the time her little sister had thrown her into a well. Every evening Josephine sat and by her presence encouraged Cora to get it all out of her system. It was disconcerting now to find that she was apparently no closer to a state of stability than she was a week ago.

As she turned she noticed that Cora appeared to be attempting to pull herself together. She was sniffing hard and rubbing her nose. 'What's he like?' she said.

'Oh, he's very good-looking,' Josephine lied. If we get her downstairs, she thought, she'll be forced to act like a sane being, and she's bound to be distracted by his personality. Bound to be.

'What's he driving?' Cora asked.

'Oh, a very nice – em – black saloon.'

'A yellow sports car,' Cora said. She was pouting.

'What?' Josephine asked, startled by the thought of a return to hysteria.

'Him. He drove.'

Oh? So what?' Josephine said. 'Come on now, we'll touch you up again and go down. Sure it'll be a giggle if nothing else.'

Cora looked at her suspiciously.

'I mean,' Josephine said, 'Just tell yourself you're going to enjoy it.'

Josephine opened the living-room door and ushered Cora in. 'Now,' she said as she stood there looking from one to the other. She felt as though she was introducing a child at a party or on her first day at school. 'Now,' she repeated, 'Sit down, Cora.'

Cora walked over and sat in the armchair opposite the television. It appeared to Josephine that she had not so much as glanced at the gentleman who was seated on the couch, his gangly legs crossed, his long Uriah Heep fingers entwined. He, meantime, had stood up briefly and sat down again.

Cora sat upright, her chubby legs together and her hands on her lap. She was examining her nails which were painted with clear varnish. Josephine was undecided as to whether to leave them alone or play the intermediary. The thought that if she left the room, Cora was likely to come trotting after her, decided her on the latter course of action.

'Well,' she said, 'This is Cora. Cora, this is Bill.'

Bill stood up again and went as if to advance towards Cora, who looked now as though she had been turned into a pillar of salt.

'Sorry we were so long,' Josephine said as she sat down on a corner of the couch on which Bill, thwarted for the second time, had reseated himself. She laughed embarrassedly. 'You know how it is.'

'That's alright.' Bill took this as a cue to relax. He spread out his legs and produced a packet of cigarettes from his pocket. He wore a permanent sly grin on his face and his movements were slippery and unconvincing. His thinning black hair was oiled and combed straight back. Late forties or early fifties, Josephine had decided the moment she opened the door to him.

'Anybody smoke?' Bill asked, offering the packet.

'No,' Josephine said. 'No, thanks, we don't.'

'Mind if I do?'

'Not at all,' Josephine said. 'You carry on.' She was at this point thinking of the girl whose body was found in the woods not too far from here. How did they know who Bill was? Was it responsible of her to allow Cora to go out with him, that's if she went at all of course. At the moment she had not the appearance of a person who was going anywhere. Then Josephine was struck again with the farce of the situation. It was not her place to allow Cora to do anything. She was, after all, only helping out, being supportive. It was too easy to find oneself taking on a role of responsibility. Maybe she had gone too far already.

'I gave them up. Used to smoke forty a day.' Cora's words were thrown across at them with the force of a ball which suddenly leaves the football pitch and arrives amongst the unprepared spectators. She was looking over at Bill for the first time. She registered no disappointment in his looks. She felt none and was only interested in imparting this piece of information about herself. Nevertheless, she had spoken and Josephine experienced a loosening-up in her muscles, so that she flopped forward slightly in relief.

'Really?' Bill's writhing frame completed several tricky movements before settling itself in a position of angular interest. 'Really?' he repeated, encouraging Cora to expand. His dark, slitted eyes peered unblinkingly, but Cora had returned to her former introspective state.

'Yes,' Josephine interposed, 'Yes, she did. Don't you think that's an achievement? To give up forty a day? Not many people can do that.'

'No, indeed,' Bill agreed. He continued looking at Cora, and Josephine found herself wondering if he could really be interested in her, especially in view of the fact that in the room there was a truly beautiful woman.

'And why, Cora, did you give them up?' he asked, in a tone of contrived interest. Cora looked at him contemptuously. 'Health,' she snapped. 'I treat my health with respect.'

Bill cast an accusatory glance at the cigarette between his fingers.

'Of course,' he said, 'You have a point. But then I believe in fate, don't you?' He blew a smoke ring towards the ceiling and watched its progress. Cora watched too, and Josephine, feeling that Cora was definitely not up to a philosophical discussion at this point, and unable to face the prospect of her launching into an account of her suicide attempts and what the psychiatrists had said, and the experience of the other patients, rose and said, 'Anybody like tea or are you going out now?'

Once out, in the pub or the park or wherever they went, they could discuss whatever they liked, or sit in silence. For all Josephine cared. All she wanted was rid of them. A cup of tea on her own, with her feet up and the television blaring, was becoming increasingly an impossible dream. 'It's getting rather late,' she added. 'I mean if you wanted to go out.'

Cora did not respond and by the expression on her face she might even have become engrossed now in the Saturday night western on the television. She might have or she might not have been aware that it was on at all. It was difficult to tell. Whatever the case, Josephine could imagine no reason why she had written in for a date in the first place. Except perhaps that she had increased by one the people who were aware of her existence.

Bill curled round and addressed Josephine. 'Are there any nice places nearby?' He smiled, making no attempt to hide the gap in his yellowing teeth.

'Well —' Josephine considered where she should send them.

'You know,' Bill enlarged, 'Intimate.'

Josephine reconsidered but before she could reply Cora piped up out of her trance. 'The Irish centre.'

Bill looked at her as if she were a child who had come out with a witticism beyond her years.

Josephine felt Cora's suggestion was nothing short of outrageous. 'Oh no, Cora,' she said, 'You don't want to go there. It's so noisy.'

Cora turned her whole body and with a look that said, 'if you don't watch I'll jump from the window', she retorted, 'It happens to be music.'

Josephine realised that she hadn't yet perfected the art of stepping in and keeping out at the right times but she was more than willing to learn.

'Of course it is,' she said. 'I'll get your coats.'

As she left the room she heard Bill saying enthusiastically, 'I've never been to one of those.' Cora did not reply.

As soon as she saw them through it Josephine closed the front door. The swiftness with which she did this was in anticipation of two possible occurrences. The first and most obvious one was that Cora would turn and bolt back in again; the second was that she would put on a lip and refuse to plant her little body in the front seat of Bill's Morris Minor, but would stomp her mules and shout, 'No, no, no.'

Josephine dashed into the room and turned up the volume on the television. She let it drown out everything. After a while she pulled back a corner of the curtain and closed her eyes in relief at the sight of the space where the Morris Minor had been. She sank into an armchair and tried to gather her thoughts.

Where was she before she had so altruistically given herself over to Cora's plight? Or to put it another way, before the landlady, who was an old friend of Cora's and had taken her in with the express purpose of looking after her, had jetted off for a holiday in the sun. Not a word had been said regarding the taking-over of responsibility for Cora. The same had been true of the cat and it had since disappeared. Before she knew it she was turning down dates, cancelling engagements, some of which had been arranged a long time ago. She was even pretending to Cora that quite suddenly all inclination to socialise had left her. She sat in, listening to the drone of Cora's voice, going over all the old ground again, inevitably reaching a crescendo during the account of her most recent, most devastating, affair with a man. And was it any wonder she had tried to commit suicide? It certainly was not. Anyone faced with such overwhelming difficulties would have done the same. And yet, Josephine was struck by the probable folly of condoning such action, one had to adopt a positive outlook. It was the only way, and it could work. 'It really could, Cora, if you give it a chance.' Occasionally she found herself resorting to such cliches as 'Look on the bright side', and once she even said, 'Every cloud has a silver lining', which made her blush and cringe, not only because of its lack of originality, but Cora could justly ask how long she was expected to wait for the silver lining to shine through.

She would hardly admit it but she was beginning to feel the strain. The strain of being helpful, meaningful, cheerful, of presenting the same controlled front, of being Cora's keeper.

She could not relax. She was edgy and unsettled. She was

going to make a cup of tea and then she changed her mind and hurried in to the phone. She needed to be reassured, to re-enter her own experience, to prove she really was Cora's opposite. It could never happen to her. She would never be disillusioned because she had decided. She was prepared for everything. And she was fortunate, yes it was true, she had natural qualities to help her on her way.

'Is Tom in? – Oh, I see – No, nothing important. Do you know where he's gone? – It's alright, I'll probably ring tomorrow – Thank you.'

There was no reason why Tom should have been in on a Saturday night. It would have been nice to have him here but it wasn't necessary. There was all the time in the world, and there was so much to fit in. Another week of Cora and it was a question of taking up where she had left off.

Ten o'clock already which meant she had between one and one-and-a-half hours before their return. Of course Cora was capable of showing up at any hour, before or after that, according to her whim. But what if there was no sign of them, say, by midnight? Would she phone the police? Or take for granted Cora was enjoying herself and had remained in his company of her own free will? And what of her ability to hold her drink? This was an unknown quantity to Josephine. She had never known her as a socialiser and mercifully she didn't drink in the house. However, it didn't require too much imagination to envisage Cora after a couple of Vodkas, tittering away if she was in a good mood, and sobbing out her woes to all and sundry if her spirits were low. Under the present circumstances Josephine was prepared for a premature return and tears.

She went up to her room to tidy through her things. She came on her collection of old photographs. She had the same settling pleasure, the unthreatened satisfaction of being reminded. The day she stood on the stones in Omeath, her green, flared summer dress a perfect match for her black wellingtons, and the family in stark remembrance. At times it seemed she was in love with what it meant. She produced it, her collection, at odd moments. It may have set her in her background. She had admitted the possibility. It may have set up barriers. But she could not deny it. It could not be denied, like beauty or truth. It was truth; and beauty in its captured distance.

Flitting from job to job was not ideal. In letters it did not sound proper. But then her main reason for coming away was to go through a series of experiences, to grow. It was not to miss important phases. It was to write the paragraphs and take them home. Eventually. She contrasted her own life with that of Cora. Cora had been walking in a maze of cul-de-sacs since childhood and there was little chance that the situation would improve. Filling Cora with optimism was the only line to take but, being honest with herself, Josephine was convinced that even if the computer spluttered up somebody with whom she could share her sad existence, their merged inadequacies would probably become impossibilities, or they would cancel each other out and leave the bemused couple floating in a neutral state.

Around eleven-thirty she was nibbling a ham sandwich in the kitchen. There was a sound like a bang on the door, duller than a knock. Edging her way round the bannisters she made her way quietly up the stairs and went into the front bedroom. Straining at the window she saw the form of Cora, hunched up on the front step. She tore down the stairs and swung open the door. Cora turned her face upwards and smiled broadly.

'Are you drunk?' Josephine said. Her first inclination was to close the door in her face. Trying to help in a situation where there were genuine problems was one thing. But barefaced drunkenness. She bent down towards Cora, who was now giggling into her chest.

'Cora, get up. Look come on in. You'll have the whole street out.'

'Let them, let them,' Cora waved dismissively towards the other houses. 'Let them all see, I don't care.' She was sitting now with her two legs sprawled wide. She looked ridiculous.

'Where's Bill?' Josephine asked. At this Cora erupted into hysterical laughter.

'Oh, Bill, Bill,' was all she said but she was waving her arm in a gesture which reminded Josephine of a farmer chasing a cow down the road.

'Was he not nice?' she asked, somewhat irrelevantly. She was on her hunkers at the door and as Cora laughed louder at this latest enquiry, she couldn't help giggling herself, as much from nervousness as amusement. But Cora's laughter was undergoing a subtle change and the tears of mirth, though identical in substance, were being transformed in purpose into tears of bitterness. Josephine was alarmed and exposed. She took Cora's arm and tried to persuade her to rise.

'Come on, Cora,' she said. 'We'll go inside and have a cup of tea and talk about it.'

At first Cora resisted, but then, like a child, overwhelmed and aware of her own vulnerability, she allowed herself to be eased up by Josephine, and together they tottered into the house. When they flopped onto the couch Cora clung to Josephine and cried and cried, until Josephine felt that she would never be extricated, that Cora was entering her person, was demanding something neither of them understood. I'm totally out of my depth, she thought. It's unfair. Unfair of Cora, unfair of Marjorie the landlady. It's unfair of the psychiatrists. Why can't they help her. 'Why can't they help you?' she shrieked at Cora, pushing with all her force, until Cora was almost vertical.

'Who?' Cora asked through the wetness.

'Clean your nose,' Josephine said, pulling a tissue from her pocket and handing it to her. Cora rubbed and wailed into the tissue, 'I want to be somebody.'

'Somebody,' Josephine repeated.

'Yes, somebody,' Cora cried and then she sobbed down into her knees, 'Nobody knows what's in me – nobody knows.'

Josephine looked at her uncertainly. Could it be that Cora possessed some higher intelligence, an unusual sensitivity of insight, that what appeared to be weakness was in fact depth? Or was she just repeating something she had heard in the psychiatric ward? At any rate, she was drunk, and that was the immediate situation to be dealt with.

'Cora,' she said, 'The best place for you is bed. You'll feel much better after a good sleep. Come on.'

Like a jelly being lifted from the fridge up onto the table,

Cora wobbled up the stairs, supported in the strength of Josephine's grip. Josephine helped her to undress down to her slip and, pulling back the bedclothes, eased her into the white comfort of her single bed. No longer crying, Cora looked up at her helplessly and as Josephine went to withdraw she held her arm and pleaded, 'Don't leave me, Josephine, don't leave me alone.'

'I won't leave you,' Josephine said. She knew her voice sounded drained and flat but Cora wouldn't notice that. She sat on the edge of the bed until Cora's rolling eyes firmly closed and did not open again. Then she checked the room quietly, making sure there were no pills, no dangerous instruments. Satisfied, she withdrew, closing the door firmly behind her. In her own room she flopped on the bed and lay for a long time staring at the cream, blank ceiling.